CONTENTS

For Sarah, Izzy & Emma

NOVEMBER ASTEROID

The first thing he noticed was the cold. The second was the paralysis.

"Can you dim the lights now please?"

The voice came from somewhere to his left. The accent was definitely an off-worlder's but not what he had heard in the orientation demo. He tried to move again, his muscles definitely responded but still he had little command over them and the attempt only seemed to bring forward his nausea.

"Dim the lights? Are you sure?"

"This man hasn't used his eyes for twenty months they will be too bright for him."

The dreadful dizziness coloured his perception and intensified an already powerful headache. He tried to bring his thoughts onto an even keel. "Twenty months? Is that all?" He watched the brightness reduce through his closed eyelids and opened them very carefully. They slowly flickered apart to reveal several spinning lights directly above him, a fuzzy indistinct face moved into view from his left and drew closer. Fingers held one of his eyes open and a bright light suddenly blinded him.

"Ouch!"

The light quickly flicked off.

"I'm sorry. I didn't realise you had reached full consciousness." The man said. "If you will give me a moment I will bring you closer to normality. I'm just going to inject a mild sedative, it should reduce your headache and settle down your sight."

The injection was rather clumsily applied to his arm but the sedative soon took effect and the headache subsided. He tried opening his eyes again and found the lights had stopped their circular motion.

"Do you know your name?" The man asked.

"Garfield Robeson." Garfield replied. "What's yours?"

"My name is Dr Bradford." Was the curt answer. He prodded the soles of Garfield's feet. "Can you feel this?"

"Yes."

"And this?" He pushed on Garfield's abdomen just below his navel.

1

"Yes."

The doctor took his small torch and looked in both of Garfield's eyes. "What is your profession?"

"I'm retired. I was a police officer." Garfield replied.

"Do you know where you are?"

"Bloxmore?" Garfield asked.

"Well, more about that later I suppose. You seem to have recovered from the sleep without any major mishaps."

"How soon will I be back to normal?" Garfield asked.

The doctor packed away some equipment out of Garfield's sight and replied without paying him any real attention. "You will recover fully over the next twenty four hours. I would recommend you do not eat until then, a small amount of water will be permissible. The paralysis will decrease over the next couple of hours. I will see you tomorrow after your night's sleep." He turned to a woman in surgical clothes, muttered something and left the room.

"Hello, I'm Dr Edwards." She said. "We'll have you moved to a bed in a private room and then there are a couple of gentlemen who would like to talk to you." She smiled and smoothed his hair back from his forehead. "I dare say you will need a haircut and a shave as well."

Garfield watched what he could from his still paralysed position, he was put onto a big comfortable trolley and wheeled through several brightly lit corridors by two bored porters. They said nothing to him and nothing to each other even in the confined lift as it carried them up to the private section on the top floor.

The room was small and contained nothing but a bed and a medical monitor that was hooked up to Garfield by an overly friendly and rather attractive nurse. "How long have we been travelling?" He enquired.

"Since Earth?" She asked.

"Yes. I thought the journey time to Bloxmore was six and a half years, but I heard the doctor say I had been asleep for only twenty months."

The door opened and Dr Edwards entered with two middle-aged men. The nurse mouthed the word 'sorry', quickly finished what she was doing and left the room.

2

"Hello Mr Robeson. I have here the two gentlemen who wish to speak with you."

Both men were well over six feet tall and dressed immaculately in pristine business suits.

"This is Councillor Barnes." She indicated to the overweight man on her left, he leaned forward and offered his hand to Garfield.

"I'm sorry councillor Mr Robeson is still in a mild state of paralysis he can't shake your hand." She said. "And this is detective Chris Venn." The detective gave Garfield a weak smile. "Well I'll leave you to it." Dr Edwards left the room.

Councillor Barnes exchanged a glance with the detective and elected to speak first. "I'm sorry we had to pull you out of your deep sleep cycle but we need your help with a very serious situation."

Garfield was not happy to hear the request and did nothing to hide his disdain.

Councillor Barnes continued regardless. "I'll be honest with you Mr Robeson, there has been the murder of a very prominent businessman on board our ship and despite the efforts of our own police service we are unable to make any headway. The council decided, with the agreement of detective Venn here, to revive you early and ask for your help."

Garfield seized the pause in Councillor Barnes speech to put a stop to the request. "I'm sorry but I'm retired. I am on my way to a quiet colony to live out the rest of my days in peace. I would like to help but I made a decision that I had seen enough of the worst of humanity and it was time to rest." He hoped that would stop the conversation there but he knew he was in for an uphill struggle. He had met a lot of councillor Barnes's in his life and if his talent for reading people continued to serve, this man would not take 'no' for an answer.

"I can offer you a very beneficial rate of pay as well as a large bonus when you capture the killer." He looked at detective Venn for help but none was forthcoming.

"I'm sorry. But I can't help you." Garfield said. "Your police service must be quite able, after all this is a city ship. What is your population? Half a million? You must have the man power."

Detective Venn interrupted. "Our police service is made up of mostly part time workers. The full time officers, like myself, have been trained on Earth but we have not had a serious crime here for several years and our training has never really been put to use. I'm afraid we are a little rusty."

"You have such a large population and no serious crime?" Garfield asked.

Detective Venn smiled. "We are in a large hollowed out asteroid travelling from star to star over a period of years. If you commit a crime where are you going to go? There's nowhere to escape to, you are effectively trapped. I'm sorry we have to ask you this but we do need your help."

Garfield could see he was not making himself clear and he was becoming angry. "How many times do I have to say no before you will listen? Please leave me alone and let me to go back into my sleep cycle."

Councillor Barnes sighed. "Very well Mr Robeson, I will ask the doctors to put you back in the fridge." He turned to leave and then stopped as if a thought had occurred to him. "You will need to recover from waking before they can put you back, perhaps a couple of days. I have just one more thing I would like to ask. Will you take a brief look at the file we have and see if you can give detective Venn some advice? You will be remunerated."

Garfield felt suddenly guilty although why he really didn't know. "Yes, Okay. I will have a look with detective Venn but I can't promise anything."

"Thank you Mr Robeson, I'll bring the file over tomorrow." Chris Venn said.

Garfield awoke to the sound of his nurse wheeling in his breakfast. He sat up and accepted the tray onto his lap, he lifted off the cover and was pleased to find a full cooked breakfast of eggs, bacon, baked beans, toast and sausages. A coffee pot and a large glass of orange juice remained on the trolley next to his bed. "Do you know when I'll be put back into the sleep cycle?" He asked.

She stopped at the door and turned to him. "Well I've never seen someone brought out of the fridge before but if you're perfectly healthy I think they can do it in about three days from now."

Chris Venn came through the door just as Garfield was starting to cut into his last sausage. His attire was a lot more casual than the day before and Garfield thought he looked more like a working detective. "Hello Mr Robeson, I have the paperwork here."

He put his brief case on the edge of the bed and produced the case file. "I'll just go and get a coffee and we can get down to it."

Garfield put the remainder of his breakfast on the trolley by his bed and opened the file. Three pages and two photographs. One image of a man lying on his back, his shirt open and a small hole in his chest just over his heart. A pool of blood had formed around the man's head. The other photograph was a series of images from a security camera showing a woman following the man along a corridor. Her wide brimmed hat concealed her face and covered her upper body down to her abdomen.

Chris Venn entered the room, took a sip of his coffee and grimaced. "Ah I see you're looking into it already." He said.

"I was expecting a little more than this." Garfield said.

"There isn't a lot more to tell you I'm afraid." Chris replied. "We can't trace the woman, we have one dubious motive and we can't even find the murder weapon."

"What was the victim's name?" Garfield asked.

"James Pierce."

"What killed him? It looks like a plasma shot to the chest but the hole is too small and there's no burning around it." Garfield lifted the picture close to his face and squinted as he examined it.

"Ah, now that is something very peculiar. He was shot with a projectile weapon."

"Pardon?"

Chris smiled. "In other words, a bullet from a firearm."

"I haven't seen one of those outside a museum. Why not just use a plasma gun?" Garfield asked.

"We have a control web routed throughout the asteroid. If somebody presses the ignition stud on a plasma weapon it will not fire unless it receives a permission code from the net and you don't get one of those without being an authorised user."

"So what is your scenario for the murder?"

"We traced his movements to a club close to his building, it's a very expensive place. Anyway, we think he picked her up there and took her to his flat where she shot him."

"How long was she in the room?"

"Three minutes."

"He still managed to get his shirt undone though." Garfield said. "And one bullet to the chest?"

"Actually there's another bullet in the skull." Chris tapped the picture just behind the man's head. "It's a very precise shot, we think it was from about five inches."

"Looks like a professional hit." Garfield could feel his fascination start to awaken. Despite himself and his decision to give up police work he was being drawn in. He had to know more and solve this puzzle. "What about motives? Who do you have on the list?" He asked.

"His business partner, Jacob Massey, stands to gain a lot from his death, apart from him there isn't anyone else. No family, no wife or ex wives. He has had a string of girlfriends but nothing really permanent." Chris sighed. "The will is made out to his brother who died two years ago."

"And what does his business partner have to say for himself?"

Chris looked slightly embarrassed. "I have interviewed him once and it was a short meeting. He is quite upset about the whole thing but it seemed to me he was more worried about himself than the victim."

Garfield wanted to know more and he decided to get further involved. "Well I believe I can't go back, 'in the fridge' as you people like to call it, for another three days so if it's okay with you I would like to interview him." Garfield said.

Chris smiled. "Sure. No problem."

Garfield Robeson and Chris Venn exited a police transit carriage and made their way up the stairs and out of the station. They emerged from the subway on a road in the financial district of the city just off the main square. The sky above them was dotted with thousands of lights laid out in expansive grid patterns that followed the curvature of the asteroid's hollowed out interior. Typical pseudo-modern office buildings lined the wide avenue and impressed an aura of extreme affluence. Powerful streetlights cast multiple shadows of the two men as they paused to get their bearings. The chilly air caused Garfield to pull his ill-fitting coat around himself and tighten the belt.

"Sorry about the clothes." Chris said. "They are all I could get at such short notice."

"Why is it so cold? I thought you would have control over the environment." Garfield said.

"Have you forgotten the name of this ship? It's not called November for nothing." Chris smiled and indicated the direction in which they should go.

Garfield followed Chris as he walked off at a fast pace. "You mean you have it like this on purpose?"

"Not on purpose. If you could look up and really see the size of this asteroid you would understand the problems with keeping a space this size warm." Chris led him to a retro style glass and steel fronted building.

Garfield looked up as they approached, the structure disappeared into the darkness above. Disembodied office lighting hung in the air above the street lights seemingly unconnected and hovering in their own right. "Why don't you light the whole interior? I would love to see the view."

"They did do when the ship was first populated, there are pictures on the postcards and in offices and, well everywhere really. The problem was that people didn't like it. Apparently the difficulty was vertigo, if you looked up and saw this tremendous distance between yourself and a city several miles above you it was a bit of a shock." Chris walked through the large glass doors, to the lifts and pushed the button.

"So you live in permanent night time?" Garfield asked.

"Yes we do. The lighting we use gives off exactly the same light as a star including whatever radiation may be necessary."

They stepped out onto the fortieth floor and approached the receptionist. "Hello we are here to see Jacob Massey, this is Garfield Robeson and I am Detective Chris Venn." He showed the receptionist his I.D.

"Mr Massey is not in yet. I will show you to his office, you can wait there." The receptionist led them through to the office of Jacob Massey's private secretary. "This is Sally she will look after you." She said.

A thirty something, bleached blond woman got up from behind her large desk and smiled at the two men. "Hello detective I wasn't expecting you. Would you gentlemen like a coffee?"

"Yes please. This is my associate Garfield Robeson." Chris motioned to Garfield.

"Hello. Black please with sugar." Garfield said.

"We are here to ask Mr Massey a few more questions. Do you know what time he will be in?" Chris asked.

"No. I'm sorry. He is usually in contact with me but the last few days have been different." Sally crossed the office to the coffee dispenser and picked up a cup. "You know he's been acting quite strangely since the murder, it's as if he's a different person. I suppose such a shock can do that to someone." She handed the two men a coffee each and returned to her desk.

"What do you mean?" Garfield asked.

"Mr Massey always had a very confident manner, sometimes he could be very intimidating if you didn't know him. But now with the Johansson offer waiting to be finalised and he is not even coming to the office I don't…" Sally paused to answer the telephone.

Chris turned to Garfield and whispered. "Sounds like a guilt trip to me."

"Maybe he's afraid he's next." Garfield replied.

"That was Mr Massey, he will not be in today. He said he is happy to see you at his home." Sally walked to the door and held it open for them. "I'm sorry I can't be more helpful." She said.

Both men exited the building and made their way to the subway.

"Can you ask someone at your office to find out what the Johansson deal is?" Garfield asked.

"Okay." Chris replied. He pulled out his portable terminal and made a quick call.

Several hundred miles of tunnels made up the subway system under the surface of the asteroid. Chris and Garfield travelled in one of the few personal carriages owned by the government through the vast network to the expensive private suburb known as October. The carriage rose up from the tunnels onto the surface as it exited the public system and followed a track running the length of a well lit golf course. Large mansion houses lined the opposite side each with its own platform and siding. The carriage slowed and pulled into the siding of a particularly imposing building. Garfield stepped out of the carriage first and looked up at the floodlit structure as Chris joined him.

"That's certainly a statement, did he have it built like that or did he buy it?" Garfield asked.

"I believe he designed it himself." Chris replied.

Garfield laughed. "Oh boy. I think he is compensating for something." He pressed the button on the intercom and was invited up the long pathway to the house.

The two large black doors that appeared reasonably sized from a distance seemed to get larger and larger as they approached. Twenty marble steps led up to the daunting entrance where a man in traditional butler's clothing awaited them.

"Good morning sirs. Mr Massey will see you in the drawing room." The butler said as he led them inside. "Can I take your jackets?" He asked.

"Thank you." Garfield said as he struggled out of his enormous coat. "How is Mr Massey this morning?" He asked.

The butler took Chris's jacket and raised his eyebrows as he accepted Garfield's coat. "Perfectly frightful sir." He replied.

They followed the servant along a wide hallway decorated with suits of armour, ancient weapons gathered mostly from oriental armies and paintings depicting massive bloody battles. The collection was arranged in such a way as to slant forwards over the guests and impose a feeling of captivity and threat.

Garfield imagined many business men led through this hall of peril before meeting Jacob Massey and giving in to any demands made of them.

At the end of the passage two suits of samurai armour stood guard with their long swords held forward ready to strike. The butler opened the door and announced their presence. Garfield and Chris entered to find the enormous darkened room illuminated only by the huge open fire in the impressive hearth. Oil paintings covered just about every inch of the walls and together with the imitation nineteenth century furniture impressed a sense of an old English mansion.

A dishevelled man in an expensive embroidered dressing gown quickly rose from his large leather chair, a small plate of toast and a coffee cup fell from his lap and clattered to the floor. He moved towards his visitors unaware his clothing had fallen open to show his shorts and fat, hairy stomach. He held out his hand to Garfield. "Hello, Jacob Massey. Pleased to meet you." His voice and posture did not portray a confident, overwhelming businessman.

9

Garfield shook his soft, limp hand. "Hello my name is Garfield Robeson, I am a detective from Earth on my way to the Bloxmore colony." He noticed a sudden shock on Jacob Massey's face. "We just want to ask a couple of questions."

"Of course. Please take a seat." Jacob replied and returned to his chair.

Chris remained standing as Garfield sat opposite Jacob in an identical piece of leather furniture. "How long had you known James Pierce?" He asked.

Jacob exhaled a slow breath. "It would be about twenty six years."

"And did you ever have arguments?" Garfield asked.

"No, not really we were very much on the same wavelength." He crossed his legs.

"Do you know any reason why someone would want him dead?"

"I've asked myself the same question but I can think of no reason or even any person who would want him dead. We were successful business men, sometimes people would get caught out by the contracts we would insist on or just lose out because we would move into an area and take over but I don't think anyone would be that angry that they would kill."

"Where were you on the night of the murder?" Garfield watched Jacob's eyes.

"I was here, alone." Jacob looked away at the ceiling.

Chris's terminal bleeped. "Excuse me." He said and left the room to take the call.

Garfield continued. "What is the Johansson offer?"

Jacob leaned forward and scratched his ankle. "Its, um, a real estate deal. We had been working hard to complete it but now I don't know if I can finish it on my own. Do you have any idea who may have done this?" Jacob Massey asked.

"Not at the moment but I'm sure you will be one of the first people to hear when we do."

Jacob Massey looked down at the fire in the large grate. His voice dropped to a whisper. "You sound very sure you will find the killer."

Garfield noticed a slight bitterness and even anger in Jacob Massey. He was regretful of something, something he feared would be uncovered.

Chris entered the room as Garfield got to his feet. "Thank you Mr Massey. We will be off now." He said.

Jacob Massey looked up at Garfield. "If there is anything I can do to help please let me know." He said.

The two men shook hands with Jacob Massey and followed the butler out to the large doors where they collected their coats. Once outside they felt free to talk.

Chris was quite animated. "The office said that the Johansson deal is enormous. I mean we're talking millions. It was all going through a company owned partly by Jacob Massey and partly by James Pierce. But the thing is Jacob had only a fifteen percent stake, most of the money from the deal goes to his partner. Unless of course something dreadful happens and then all the money goes to you know who, Jacob Massey."

Garfield smiled. "You know, that guy in there was so transparent, he was definitely hiding something. Now all you have to do is find the woman and link her to Massey." He said.

"Yeah, sure, piece of cake." Chris replied.

Garfield lay still on his hospital bed, tired and hungry after going without food for twenty-four hours. His small trip into the business world of the November asteroid had kept him awake most of the night. He had been seized by the chase and ran through the various possible scenarios for the murder of James Pierce. The one person that he kept coming back to was the woman. She had killed as efficiently as any professional he had come across but he couldn't imagine a working assassin would give up six and a half years and cross to a quiet colony just for one hit. Unless of course she had been paid a very large sum of money but then her profile would have been checked before boarding and anybody suspected of that kind of occupation would not have been allowed on the ship. He couldn't imagine somebody becoming that professional without being noticed and recorded somewhere in a police databank.

Dr Edwards entered the room. "Mr Robeson we will be taking you down to be prepared for the fridge soon. I'm going to give you a sedative now and the porters will collect you in ten minutes." She turned and took a syringe from a tray by the bed. "Could I have your arm please?"

"Oh, no, please stop." It was Chris Venn. "I'm sorry Garfield but we still need you."

Dr Edwards looked between the two men and then at the syringe. "Mr Robeson?" She asked.

"Oh bugger, alright, alright I'm coming. Dr, I hope to see you soon and have the pleasure of you jabbing me with that thing." Garfield flipped the cover off himself. "Would somebody pass me those trousers?" He asked.

Garfield followed Chris into the private transit carriage and sat opposite him. "Well, what has happened?" He asked.

Chris sat forward. "We had a missing person report on a doctor in the east end of the city. After running the usual checks it was confirmed he is actually missing, which is quite a trick if you consider we are in a spaceship."

Garfield was getting a little impatient. "And what has this to do with the murder inquiry?" He asked.

"The missing person is James Pierce' personal doctor, Michael Clark. And he hasn't been seen since the night of the murder."

"Ah, I see. So now we have a possible double murder. How difficult would it be to hide a body on this ship?"

"Not too difficult I suppose. But somebody would have to be pretty careful moving it. The east end is an expensive district covered in security cameras. If you wanted to move a body without being seen and avoid the building's internal cameras you would have to disguise it as something innocuous."

Garfield could feel his old excitement growing again and he hated himself for it. A man had died and another was missing, possibly dead, and all he could do was revel in the chase, the cat and mouse contest between himself and the murderer. He was trying to get away from this awful pleasure he had in the macabre but once again he was snared. "Where are we going now?" He asked.

"We called his clinic to verify the last time he was seen there and when the nurse checked his office she said it looked like there had been a fight. I've sent a couple of officers over there and we are going to meet them."

The two men alighted the carriage in the large underground Brentford hospital station. Their carriage quickly moved off into a parking siding leaving them to walk the busy platform to the entrance. Four separate tracks entered the cavernous concourse leading to a central hub where paramedics collected incoming accident and emergency patients. A red strobe flashed above a door marked east and Garfield had to dodge a fast moving trolley rushing alone to the middle platform. A white carriage marked with a large red cross pulled in to the siding and was met by the single minded trolley.

Garfield and Chris entered the building through two large glass doors and followed the signs to the Organ Replacement Department on the fourth floor. A nurse directed them through to a room with a police guard. Garfield stopped just inside the door and viewed the scene. Two men in police uniform stood to one side talking and sharing a laugh. A chair lay on its back behind the desk and the floor was covered with pieces of paper and items from the desktop. Books littered the area of floor in front of a tall wooden bookcase next to a broken lamp.

Chris approached the two uniformed policemen. "Garfield this Dan Simpson and Clive Brown." He turned to Dan Simpson. "Did you bring the scanners?" He asked.

"Yes we did." Simpson replied. He handed the device to Chris who opened the case and reviewed the data.

Garfield joined him. "Certainly looks like something happened here. Are you getting any DNA traces on the scan?" He asked.

"Yes." Chris sighed. "Quite a lot actually, but if he was seeing several patients in here every day you would expect that. I'll get the guys to call up a list of clients and staff here and see if we pick out any uncertainties." He handed the scanner back to Simpson. "Transmit the data to the office straight away." He said.

Garfield walked around the room and looked for anything suspicious, the paperwork on the floor looked like normal patient notes and there was nothing unusual in the desk drawers or behind it. A small hole in the bookcase caught his eye. "Can you give me a hand to move this?" He asked.

The two officers joined Garfield and Chris and moved the bookcase forward enough for Garfield to get behind it. He looked between the

13

small hole in the bookcase and a hole in the wall. He picked at it and a small metal object fell into his palm. A confident smile shaped his lips and he held it up for Chris to see. "What does this look like to you?" He asked.

"A bullet from a projectile weapon." Chris replied. He turned to his two colleagues. "Get me the closed circuit footage for this hospital on the night of the murder and get that DNA list as soon as possible." He said.

Simpson opened his terminal and started a call to the security office.

Garfield handed the bullet to Chris. "If we can place that woman here on the night of the murder and trace her DNA we should be able to track her down quite easily."

Dan Simpson disturbed them. "Sir, sorry to interrupt but the security office has said the closed circuit records we need have been deleted. They said that it was highly unlikely to be a computer malfunction. They are looking for an explanation."

Garfield shook his head. "Find out who could do that." He said. "I'd like to talk to the head nurse who was on duty that night. Is she here?" He asked.

"Yes we have her in a room down the hall." Simpson led Garfield and Chris out of the room.

Emily Nichols sat by herself in the corner of the small waiting room and dabbed at her red swollen eyes. Her attempt at a brave smile as Garfield and Chris entered the room revealed perfect gleaming teeth.

Garfield fetched a drink from the water dispenser in the corner and handed it to her. "I'm sorry to put you through this but we need to ask some questions. Remember this is still only a missing person case." Emily burst into tears again and Garfield took the cup back while she pulled fresh tissues from a box.

"I know, I'm sorry." Emily composed herself and looked at both Garfield and Chris. "OK. I'm ready." She said.

"When was the last time you saw Dr Clark?" Chris asked.

"I finished up in the lab at six o'clock and went to his office to let him know I was leaving." She said.

"And how did he seem to you? Was he nervous or excited? Was there anything about him that seemed unusual?"

14

"He looked up from his desk and smiled. He said, 'I'll see you tomorrow'. That was it."

"Can you tell me what Dr Clark specialised in?" Garfield asked.

"He was head of organ replacement and clone research." She replied.

"How much time did he spend between the two?"

"Most of his time was spent in the research lab but I'd say he would spend twenty percent of his time supervising the growing of cloned organs." She picked a fresh tissue from the box and blew her nose.

"We know the murder victim, Michael Pierce, was one of his private patients. Can you tell us exactly what Dr Clark was doing for him?" Garfield asked.

"Well I'm not supposed to say but he was growing a replacement liver for him, it was a standard procedure. Mr Pierce had a damaged liver from too much drink and this was the easiest way to solve the problem."

Garfield collected a fresh drink for Emily. "And what about the clone research, how far had he got with that work?" He asked.

"We can grow a full adult body in three months with accelerated growth. Michael, I mean Dr Clark, was trying to work out a way to transfer the mind state out of an old body and into a young one. He saw it as the next step in organ replacement, just reject the whole old body and buy a new one."

"Had he succeeded in the mind transfer?" Chris asked.

"No, we were close though. Now I don't know if anyone will be able to carry on his work." She pulled a fresh tissue from the box and blew her nose.

"Was Jacob Massey a patient of Dr Clark's?"

"No, I'm sorry I've never heard of him."

"Thank you Emily." Garfield said.

Chris waited until she had left the room before speaking. "What do you think?" He asked.

"Well I don't think she can tell us anything that would interest us. Can we go to the police station and review the results from the scanner?" Garfield asked.

In the Brentford hospital lobby Garfield and Chris exited the lift with the two uniformed officers. They passed through the

15

Accident and Emergency reception on route to the private police siding. The busy receptionist was struggling to book in a group of injured rugby players and Garfield smiled as he recalled a few injuries of his own during his time with his local club. His eyes caught sight of a young woman barely out of her teens watching him as he walked towards the exit. She had her hands tucked into the pockets of her open ankle length black coat. A long woollen scarf draped around her neck and over a black polo neck jumper. Garfield noticed between her short skirt and suede boots a number of bruises on her bare legs. He looked back at her face and was held for a moment by her intense, almost angry stare. A bleeping on Chris' terminal refocused his attention and he stopped to allow him to answer the call.

"Are you sure?" Chris asked. "OK. Thank you. We will be back with you in thirty minutes can you have the results from the hospital scanner ready for us? Oh, and can you get hold of the closed circuit recordings for outside the hospital on the night of the Pierce murder?" He turned to Garfield and sighed. "Jacob Massey has wound up his business interests and pulled out of the Johansson deal."

"If he has pulled out of that deal there would be no point to have killed Pierce. That was our prime motive theory. If Massey didn't have him killed then who did?" Garfield asked.

"It may be he's scared off the whole thing and trying to get out of looking guilty." Chris replied.

"That doesn't sound like the confident Massey we were told about." Garfield said.

The carriage stopped outside the police station at one of the several sidings. Garfield stepped out and viewed the building's stark exterior, he wondered if local government anywhere in the galaxy would ever design an attractive building. The interior buzzed with the usual high pace police activity Garfield was well used to. Chris showed him into a large briefing room. A sizeable display screen took up the wall opposite a long table. He sat with Chris as a middle-aged woman entered and loaded a memory disk into the computer beneath the screen.

"Hello Chris. Is this the man from the fridge?" She smiled, approached the table and held out her hand to Garfield.

He half stood and shook her hand. "Hello, Garfield Robeson." He introduced himself.

"Janet Manning." She replied. She picked up a small remote control, the lights dimmed and the screen activated. Four views of the outside of the hospital entrance appeared each from a different high angle. "We have reviewed the recordings using both active sprite recognition and body template cross referencing using the footage from outside James Pierce' flat as the source material. On the night of the murder we have found images of a woman leaving the hospital that match the search criteria to eighty eight percent." Janet pointed the remote control at the screen and the four different images began moving. "She is wearing the same dress as the pictures from the source material but not the hat and we have a good view of her face." The video paused and Janet used the remote to bring one of the four views up to take over the whole screen. A red square appeared around a distant figure and the picture zoomed in.

"Damn it!" Garfield exclaimed. "I saw her today, at the hospital as we were leaving. She had different clothes but it was definitely her."

"Are you sure?" Chris asked.

"She had bruised knees, I didn't think anything of it. We were in a hospital and an injured person doesn't seem out of place. She stared at me, I caught her eyes as we walking out." Garfield said.

"You have footage of her leaving but not entering?" Chris asked.

"I have found footage of her coming back to the hospital later that evening and then leaving again only a few minutes afterwards. I ran a search through the whole week to see when she first arrived and she doesn't appear at the hospital at any point. It's as though she was born there." Janet said.

The door opened, Dan Simpson entered and handed Janet a memory disk. She took the first one out of the computer and slipped in the new one. "We have the results of the DNA scans." He said. The screen filled with an extensive list of names, the file scrolled down until two DNA samples appeared flashing red. One of the samples had no name next to it and the other had the name Jacob Massey.

"Jacob Massey? Didn't Dr Clark's nurse say that he was not a patient?" Chris asked.

"Yes. In fact she said she had never heard of him. What about that other sample? There is no name. Don't you have the DNA on file of every person on this ship?" Garfield asked.

"Yes and that's only half of the puzzle." Dan Simpson replied. "Our standard recognition software couldn't identify the DNA but when I did a more thorough analysis I got the name Jacob Massey. I ran the check three times, all had the same outcome. Now here's the real weird thing, the computer says that the DNA this person belongs to is female."

Garfield looked at Chris. "A clone?" He suggested.

"You think that woman is a female clone of Jacob Massey?" Chris asked.

"What if Jacob Massey paid Dr Clark to grow a female version of himself and transfer his mind into it. He could then go and kill James Pierce with no chance of being recognised." Garfield said.

"But that doesn't quite fit the facts, the woman is still running around out there, Jacob Massey is in his house, Dr Clark is missing and he hadn't perfected the mind transfer technique." Chris said.

Dan Simpson interrupted. "One more thing, the head of security at the hospital called. They've tracked down who deleted the closed circuit recordings from the night of the murder. It was Dr Clark."

"It doesn't make much sense" Garfield replied. "He is missing presumed murdered. Which would make him a victim. So why would he erase the recordings? I think we need to interview Mr Massey again." He said.

"Why Massey?" Chris asked.

"I want to know what he was doing with Dr Clark that night and why he has pulled out of his businesses." Garfield replied.

Garfield and Chris stepped out of the transit carriage and stopped for a moment to look at the imposing Massey residence. Not one room was illuminated. Garfield pushed the button on the intercom and waited for the reply. "Did you hear if he was leaving town at all?" He asked.

"No, I didn't." Chris replied.

18

With no answer coming from the intercom Garfield pushed the gate and found it unlocked. He glanced at Chris and walked through towards the building. As they approached a dull red glow became visible through the drawing room window, it flickered and danced sending momentary shadows across the glass.

The large black doors were slightly ajar, Garfield pushed one open. The light from the exterior lit the hallway and cast their long shadows across the crumpled heap of the butler's body. Chris pulled his plasma pistol from his belt as Garfield checked the man's neck for a pulse. He lifted his hand to find it covered in blood. Chris moved ahead of Garfield and they made their way down the imposing weapon laden hallway. A man's sobbing suddenly stopped them in their tracks, through the open door to the drawing room the fireplace shed a shimmering crimson glow illuminating the suits of samurai armour in their menacing lifelike pose. Garfield crept forward to get a better view of what was happening in the room.

Jacob Massey was on his knees in front of the young woman who was holding a firearm to his head. "I'm sorry. I didn't think you would kill him." His pathetic sobs punctuated his speech. "If I had known I would never have done this, I would have done what you asked."

"You will transfer me back or I swear I will kill you." She said.

An expression of terrified desperation grabbed Jacob Massey's features. "But what about me? Where will I go? If you have this body back I have nowhere to be transferred to. I will die." He cried.

"You should have thought of that before you tried to betray me." She smiled. "You can have this body, you were so happy to condemn me to it, now it is your turn."

Chris joined Garfield at the door and brought his plasma pistol forward to point it at the woman. "I'm going in." He said. Before Garfield could respond Chris went through the door and aimed his weapon at her. "Police. Don't move." He shouted.

The woman twisted quickly and fired a shot at Chris that sent him diving for cover. Jacob Massey threw himself on the floor as the woman jumped over the leather chair and disappeared through the opposite door.

Chris handed Garfield his plasma pistol. "You're probably more used to this than me. Don't worry you're authorised to use it. I'm going to call in some help." He picked his terminal out of his pocket and stood next Jacob Massey. "I'll watch him." He said.

Garfield crouched down by the door the woman had exited through. He looked out along the corridor and saw a flash as the firearm discharged. A part of the doorframe above his head shattered and a spray of splinters showered his back. He fired the plasma pistol at the area from where he saw the flash and heard the sound of running high-heeled shoes. The snicking sound of handcuffs being locked caught his attention and he looked back to see Chris securing Jacob Massey to a large table.

"I'm going after her." Garfield said.

"There should be some people here to help us in a few minutes. Good luck." Chris replied.

Garfield reached out in the darkness and found the wall opposite the doorway, he felt his way along until he accidentally kicked something small with his left foot. He reached down and found one of the woman's shoes. He moved forward being careful to make as little noise as possible, when he reached the end of the corridor he looked through the door to his right and saw the silhouette of the woman move across a window. The sharp crack of the plasma discharge accompanied a pin fine beam of light as it crossed the room and cut into the her shoulder. She cried out and tripped over onto the floor, the firearm clattered across the room. Garfield ran forward and grabbed her hands. He rolled her onto her front and pulled her hands together behind her back.

She howled at the pain in her shoulder. "Let me go or I'll make sure you never work again." She said.

"You know, that was my plan right from the start." He replied. He picked her up and pushed her out of the room and along the corridor.

Chris looked up from Jacob Massey as Garfield entered with the woman.

"He did the murder, I didn't know he was going to kill someone. I had nothing to do with it." Jacob Massey pleaded.

"Shut up you useless moron." The woman shouted at him.

"What do you mean, he did the murder?" Garfield asked.

20

The woman interrupted before Jacob Massey could answer. "Don't listen to him he's obviously deluded." She said.

Jacob Massey talked desperately and quickly. "My name is Michael Clark, Dr Michael Clark. I work at Brentford hospital, you can check on me. She is Jacob Massey I moved his mind into her, she's a clone."

The woman tried to get up from her seat. "I told you he was raving mad." She said.

Garfield put his hand up in front of her and she sat down. "We have already interviewed people at the hospital, we are well aware of the cloning technology. But Dr Clark why did you transfer yourself into Jacob Massey?" He asked.

"Money. It may sound stupid but when I saw the chance to leave my job and just take all that cash I thought why not? I didn't think he was a killer. I thought if and when he turned up as a woman and claimed to be Jacob Massey I could just say she was a crazed stalker." He sighed and looked at the floor. "I'm so sorry." He said.

"Wouldn't your cloning technique make you rich?" Garfield asked.

"No. The patents are all owned by the hospital. I am only on a wage."

"I am not Jacob Massey." The woman said.

"We will take you both into custody and examine the evidence." Garfield said.

The woman laughed. "What are going to do? Arrest me? What for?" She asked.

"You attempted to kill me tonight and evade arrest. We have film of you at James Pierce' house and at the hospital as well as your DNA in Dr Clark's office. Don't worry we have enough to hold you." Chris said.

Garfield Robeson became gradually aware of his cold paralysis and his first thought, his first hope was that he was not yet at Bloxmore colony. After his police work with Chris Venn he had once again tasted the awful excitement of a murder case and become stained by his craving for the hunt. Like an addict now on a downward slope he needed more.

21

The needle stabbed lightly at his arm and Garfield opened his eyes to see a portly nurse. "Hello Mr Robeson. Welcome to Bloxmore." She said.

Garfield struggled to speak and managed only a gravelly whisper. "Can I ask you a question?"

"Of course." She said.

"Can you tell me where the nearest police station is?"

REPARATION

This was his best chance so far, well if he was honest it was the only chance he had had in six months but that didn't mean it wasn't a good one. He knew Captain Balucci was around here somewhere he just had to carry on looking and keep his wits together. He owed it to himself and most of all he owed it to Gary. If he had kept them where they should have been and not gone off after of an easy target they wouldn't be in this mess. He felt a wash of sadness from the other man's soul.

Once a month the independent ore carriers inhabited the landing bay and turned it into a bustling, congested bazaar. Traders from most of the local governments and corporations came with virtual wallets filled with virtual money to buy the precious Mallenite ore from the independents. Most of the autonomous owner-Captains were perfectly above board in all their dealings but he was looking for a reprobate, a dubious Captain who didn't mind taking on crew even with the most shadowy past.

Axel Fendar spotted Captain Luigi Balucci by a drinks dispenser. The Captain kicked it twice and checked the tray. There was no drink. He proceeded to swear at the machine in an impressive display of both vocabulary and profanity.

Axel introduced himself. "Hello Captain Balucci. My name is Axel Fendar I heard you are looking for crew for your ship."

Captain Balucci looked Axel in the eye and then regarded him from head to toe. "I have no need for cleaners or labourers on board my ship." He took his cigar from between his lips, leaned forward and spat a mouthful of dark drool at Axel's feet.

"I have a class one pilot licence…" Captain Balucci walked away before Axel could finish his sentence. He chased after him. "I have the certificates here." Axel offered his terminal. "You can see they are legitimate. I heard you need a navigator…"

The Captain turned and grabbed Axel by the throat. "I do not take failures onto my ship." He replied with a gravely Italian accent obviously stained by far too many cigars. He released Axel and waited for him to leave. "What are you waiting for? Go. I do not have time to waste."

Axel may have fallen into a dishevelled image of his former self since his discharge but he still retained some of his self-confidence. "I have money, it is all I have but I would pay for transport as well as working my way."

Captain Balucci's eyes sparkled at the mention of money. "Money? How much? Where would you get money from?" He gestured at Axel with a derisory wave.

"It is my discharge payment." Axel replied.

The Captain laughed. "You were discharged? Ah now you sound more like my kind of man. They threw you out did they?"

"It was an honourable discharge." Axel was on the defensive.

"You and I both know there is no such thing as an honourable discharge." He put his arm around Axel's shoulder. "Why do you want to go back into space?" He asked.

"I have a debt to repay a fallen comrade." Axel replied. The other man's soul shimmered at the limits of his awareness. Captain Balucci considered for a moment. "Believe it or not I was once also a military man. I do not want to take your discharge money but I am not a rich man and bills have to be paid. It is true my navigator has left me. Did you have proper navigation training or that silly little course all pilots have to suffer just to get their licence?"

"I passed both grade two and three." Axel offered.

"Come with me, I think I can use you." Captain Balucci walked off in the direction of the landing bay.

The trading vessel Modest Sophia did not impress Axel in any way. Captain Balucci described the ship as his first and last wife. It was a basic loader class interstellar freighter and had seen more than its fair share of work.

Captain Balucci opened a small access flap underneath the main body of the craft and typed a code into the key pad. Nothing happened. He turned and smiled at Axel and typed again, still nothing. The flap closed as Captain Balucci uttered a few choice swear words. He pulled his terminal from his pocket and opened a link to the bridge. "Monica. Please open the door the keypad is not working again." After a loud mechanical clunk and a worrying grinding noise the entrance gantry lowered from the fuselage.

Axel followed Captain Balucci onto the bridge. The equipment comprised of various pieces obviously taken from a large variety of different craft. Optical wiring hanging in a haphazard web from the ceiling connected apparatus all over the bridge. Several air conditioning units whined above him amongst the only partially functioning lighting. He was a little surprised to find an all female crew.

"My fellow crew mates, I would like to introduce you to our new navigator, Ahmed Pendal." Captain Balucci said.

"Axel Fendar." Axel corrected.

Captain Balucci continued. "Yes of course. I am sure you would all like to welcome Ahmed on board. We are leaving immediately. Prepare the ship." He turned and left Axel facing the three women.

They looked at Axel with either distrust or suspicion.

The woman by the pilot seat walked over to Axel. "I am Olivia, I am the pilot." Axel had to concentrate to find his way through her thick Italian accent. "This is Emily our engineer and this is Martina our systems specialist." She pointed to each woman in turn.

Martina walked forward and shook his hand. "You are our forth navigator in two months, how did Luigi find you?"

"I found him. I need the work." Axel looked about the bridge for the navigator station.

"Work? You'll get that alright." She said.

The craft lifted off the landing bay and passed through the environment shield into vacuum. Olivia pushed the thrusters hard and accelerated out of the gravity well with little regard for the planetary speed limit. Axel noticed that at least the Captain kept the engines in perfect working order.

"Axel can I have the course plot please?" Olivia asked.

"Yes one moment, I am finishing the inputting now." He quickly checked the numbers on his display and sent them to the pilot station. "It's coming over now." He said.

"Emily is the gravity generator over seventy five percent?" Olivia called out.

"Ninety three percent." She replied.

Axel couldn't understand why Olivia was shouting out these questions and not just looking at her displays. He turned in his chair and looked over her shoulder, only one of her displays was functioning. He sucked in a deep breath and wondered if he had made the right choice of ship.

"Gravity jump in ten seconds." Olivia's voice resonated out of the P.A. system.

There was the slight sense of movement that indicated a gravity jump.

Emily turned to face the bridge. "OK, first jump impression completed. We will need about eight hours now to recharge the inducers."

Axel checked their position and locked the system. "Can someone show me where my cabin is?" He asked.

#

The magnificent bloom of escaping craft was only matched by the astonishing splendour of the exploding alien war ship. Each of the thousand tiny vessels moving away from the catastrophic detonation left a stunning plasma trail in its wake.

The powerful sight compelled Axel to gaze open mouthed through his window, countless energy trails filled his field of vision in an incredible firework display. "They've done it!" He shouted.

"We have to destroy the escape pods." Gary Summ, Axel's co-pilot said. He changed the calibration on the targeting computer to seek out the smaller vessels.

The Human armada leapt forward on an intercept course for the cloud of lightly armed alien craft. The tremendous acceleration pushed Axel into his seat and only served to heighten his excitement. There was little or no chance of harm coming from the encounter and if any emotion gained control of him it was happiness. The war was almost at an end and Axel was fighting in the final battle. For six years he had fought, suffered and hated but now he could finally leave all that behind. The alien Theast invasion had failed and the human race was victorious.

"They're forming ranks and changing course for us." Gary said.

"Bring the main weapons group online and set the secondary unit on standby, when we get close activate them both but control the main groups' targeting yourself. Don't let any of them get away." Axel disengaged the auto-pilot and took control of the vehicle. His main display lit up with red warning icons as the aliens fired their weapons. Axel looked out of the window to his right and

27

saw the storm of hostile energy fill the void in front of the Human fleet.

Gary reached over the control panel and switched on the energised hull shielding. The pitiful alien barrage failed to breach the defence and dissipated into the surrounding vacuum.

"I'm activating the argon energy beam." Gary triggered the powerful weapon and sliced through an enemy craft. The hull split in two and fell back from the battle.

For the first time in his military career Axel saw an alien with his own eyes. The flailing body drifted away from the shattered craft and joined the wreckage of combat.

Gary picked out his targets and fired on them one by one as the huge number of aliens crossed the expanse and neared the wall of Human fire. He brought up the main weapons group targeting scanner and initiated a class one fire pattern. The two man raider class battle craft rocked as the violent energy discharge exited the combustion generators. The sweep of energy had a catastrophic effect on the offensive alien vessels. "They're suicidal. Why don't they turn back? They must know they stand no chance." He said.

Axel shouted as the alien menace drew near. "Here they come. Keep your eyes open its going to get pretty dense." He tightened his grip on the joystick as the two opposing forces collided in swarm of hostile fire. The secondary weapons group fired automatically picking out alien craft with minute blasts threaded between the fast moving Human vessels. "Gary. Hold your fire until you can be sure of a target the field's too dense for mistakes."

Adrenalin fuelled Axel's intense concentration as he searched for a viable quarry.

The theatre of battle opened up and Gary fired on a nearby alien craft. The blast wave from the resulting explosion struck the ship and sent it tumbling out of control. "We've lost secondary weapons." He shouted.

Axel contained the twisting and sighted an alien out beyond the main battle. He pointed it out to Gary. "I'm going after the alien out there, fire on him as soon as you get the shot."

The alien craft was already damaged and was twisting violently through a long arc. A hole in the hull allowed a gaseous escape that trailed behind in a haphazard spiral. Random bright flashes sparkled amongst the vapour painting a glistening trail.

Thrusters around the circumference of the vessel fired in a rapid sequence as the pilot struggled to bring it under control.

Gary fired the plasma canon and missed the target. "Sorry." He said. He fired again and caught the alien just on the edge of its fuselage.

Instead of causing any real damage to the craft it righted the twisting and the alien regained control. It accelerated at a tremendous rate and curved around behind the Human ship.

Axel pulled hard on the joystick to bring them on a pursuit course and give Gary a decent shot. As the alien came into view he realised the enemy had chosen to do the unthinkable. He hit the eject button and pushed the back of his head into the headrest as the small two man cockpit blasted away from the main body of the ship. The shocking gee force pushed the air from his lungs and put a painful pressure on every part of his body.

The alien craft rammed into the Human ship and breached the reactor housing. A massive blast wave expanded from the collision and pummelled the ejected cockpit. The resulting strength of the explosion sent the cockpit into a violent spin. Axel lost consciousness.

A slow confused awareness came to him, he was disembodied and floating through a vast darkness. The impenetrable black expanse implied a glimpse of eternity his mind could barely grasp. A light winked on. The distance between himself and the illumination was impossible to guess but it seemed as if it was growing in brightness. Several colours shimmered across the distance and connected with Axel. A hint of thought drifted through his mind as if it was trying to impart a message. It occurred to him it was getting nearer and he watched it, unable to move, unable to avoid the approaching question. It struck him at great speed and seized him in an overwhelming embrace. He was suffocating under the stress of the other more powerful mind. Axel had no strength to protest and it joined with him to become a part of his own consciousness. A sudden powerful need to give way to oblivion took hold of him and he passed into a void of dreamless sleep.

#

Axel shifted himself onto his back and gazed up at the filthy ceiling. His sore eyes caused him little irritation, similarly his sadness had now become only a foundation upon which any other emotion must sit. Tiredness was something he had become accustomed to over the last few weeks. Sleep is not easy to come by when another soul inhabits your subconscious. It's subtle continuous background noise harassed his thoughts and kept him permanently aware he could never be alone.

Soon he must take control of the ship and direct it to Theast the veiled planet of his companion's dreams. He owed it to the man to take him to the lake of hope and free him to its waters. A knock at the door dragged him from his thoughts. "Hello?" He shouted.

The door opened and Olivia peered around to look at him. "We are going to make the next jump in an hour or so. If you want to eat you had better come now." She said.

Axel thought for a moment and decided he would need some energy for the coming day. The crew might not respond well when they realise he has taken them off their route. "Breakfast sounds like a good idea." He replied.

Olivia led him to the small galley. The only food on offer was the awful frozen meals he had become familiar with in the military. He picked out a box of bacon, eggs, sausages and toast and put it in the heater. It popped out a moment later, the dreadful plastic smell of the food did not arouse his appetite. He sat at the table with rest of the crew and opened the box. "Does the Captain not eat with us?" He asked.

"You won't see much of him, he likes his drink a little too much." Martina said.

"Yeah and few substances he should have grown out of by his age." Olivia added.

"So why do you stay with him?" Axel asked.

"He has great contacts and he pays big bonuses when the contracts are fulfilled. Anyway I prefer to work without one of those Captains who is always looking over your shoulder and always telling you things could be done better." Martina replied. "Here we can do what we like as long as we get the job done."

Axel looked around the galley, it was the cleanest room he had seen so far.

Martina watched him and laughed. "I know the ship looks bad but it runs just fine." She checked the time and got up from her seat. "The inducers should be charged now, we ought to make the next jump."

Axel took his seat at the navigator's display, closed his eyes and allowed the other man's soul to come forward. Direct communication was never possible but he did get a sense of what the other man wanted to share. The co-ordinates for the veiled planet made themselves known through this odd connection and Axel input them into the computer. A green icon flashed indicating the location was empty and a safe area to jump into. If the planet was on the star charts he should have seen a red icon. He adjusted the co-ordinates to bring the ship's emergence point away from the planet to a safe distance.

"Axel have you got the co-ordinates?" Olivia asked.

"Yes, they're ready." After he forwarded them to her he took a memory crystal from his pocket and loaded his stealth software into the computer.

"Emily the gravity generator level please?" Olivia called out.

"Ninety percent." She replied.

"Gravity jump in ten seconds." Olivia confirmed in the P.A. system.

There was the slight sense of movement that indicated a gravity jump.

Emily looked over at Axel, she appeared slightly confused. "I charged the inducers for a sixty two light year jump. We've just jumped over one hundred and forty light years. The inducers are fried. Axel? What have you done?"

Olivia checked their position on her one working display. "We're outside the perimeter and into Theast space. Axel either you're a terrible navigator or..." She paused as she realised he had brought them here on purpose. "You want to be here."

Axel accessed his software and started the programme. All the displays on the bridge shut down as the software took control of the ship and locked the crew out. "I'm sorry." He said. "But I have to get to the surface of that planet." He pointed out of the window.

Martina stood up and glared at Axel. "You're not going anywhere. Release the ship." She demanded.

31

"When I am safely on the surface I will send you the codes and the ship will be released." He edged toward the door. Olivia and Martina moved to stop him, he rushed for the exit but they blocked him. He pushed forward and found their attempts to stop him weaker than expected. Emily grabbed his collar and pulled him, her strength was not great but combined with the others they managed to force him over backwards to the floor.

"Call the Captain." Emily shouted.

Martina reached for the intercom and at that moment Axel rolled onto his front and pushed forward through the door. He struggled to his feet and ran forward as the two women came after him. He turned a corner, spun around and stopped. Emily came into sight just ahead of Olivia. Axel brought his fist up and jabbed her sharply on her nose. She stumbled and blocked Emily for a second as Axel ran away down the small passage. Olivia's knees gave way under her and she collapsed in front of Emily.

"You son of a bitch." Emily shouted as she stepped over Olivia.

Axel reached the small lifeboat and activated the airlock. As the door opened he turned to face Emily. He raised his fists and returned her intense stare.

Emily backed up the passageway, she had obviously lost her will to fight. Axel was much taller than her and she was no match for him. "What are you doing? This planet is not even on the charts." She said.

Axel stepped into the airlock. "I owe a debt to a friend who died with me in the war."

"Died with you?" She asked. Emily was exasperated.

Axel paused, he didn't want to leave the crew without explaining at least something of what he was doing. "We were in the final battle, an alien escape pod rammed our ship. I survived but my co pilot died." Axel checked the airlock control for a green light. "I don't know what happened exactly but I carry his soul within me and the only way to release him is to visit this planet." Axel perceived a sense of urgency from the soul. He closed the airlock and opened the opposite door to enter the escape pod. The straps came loose from the wall as he tried to secure himself in the pod. He looked around at the interior and with a large amount of trepidation he hit the launch control. The explosive bolts fired and the pod drifted away from the ship. The moment the pod was free the artificial gravity ceased and Axel lifted from his seat. A timer on the wall counted down to the ignition of the small rocket that would direct the pod to the planet. He grasped the ends of the straps and closed his eyes. The rocket fired and angled the pod on a course for the atmosphere. Axel was thrown against the inside of the cabin by the sudden gee force. The windows glowed a deep fluorescent red as the pod buffeted against the atmosphere, intermittent creaking noises resounded around Axel lending him an anxiety he had not felt since the morning of a battle.

The pod raced headlong into an ever increasing atmospheric pressure, Axel peered out to get his first glimpse of the planet. He was racing over a large ocean and ahead of him just in view was the only land mass on the globe. The pod marked its course across the alien sky with a trail of angry plasma. The main rocket fuel ran out and the engine was automatically ejected, when it had fallen away three small rocket motors ignited below the pod and slowed its descent. Axel relaxed after the systems had all worked correctly and took hold of the small direction control. He tried to sense the other soul and gain some idea of the direction he should take, it came to him in a flash, the exact location in a perfect link more powerful and dynamic than he had experienced before. He brought the pod on a southerly track and tried to get a view of the site through the small display, his height had decreased considerably and the continent below was now racing underneath him in a dirty green blur. He passed over a set of low, snowy peaks and reduced his speed to three hundred kph. A massive jungle was now laid out before him, the soul shimmered in the recesses of his consciousness, the lake was now close, the journey was almost over. The stunning expanse of the lake was suddenly below him, it appeared from amongst the mass of foliage as a blue haven cut out of the seemingly foul, tangled rain forest mess.

Axel found a small area free of the dense undergrowth and suffered an untidy landing as the automatic pilot dumped the pod on the ground. He activated the communications beacon and initiated the transmission of the codes to the ship in orbit. A few seconds later he received the recognition response from his stealth software and confirmation it had disengaged. The display lit up and he found the face of Captain Balucci looking at him. Axel cut the connection as the stream of foul language commenced.

Two emergency environment suits filled the small locker under the seat and Axel proceeded to test each piece of equipment and clothing in a search for a full functioning set. One of the suits was obviously built for Captain Balucci as the waist size was far too large for Axel. The other was cut for the female form but even so it fit him better than the enormous bulk of the Captain's suit. After he had put it on and attached the one half full oxygen tank he sealed the helmet over his head and asked the pod to connect to the small processor and verify its status. A sixty three percent operating status was the reply, Axel sighed and pressed the release catch on the small hatch.

Axel struggled to pull himself head first through the small exit and tumbled in a heap on the rocky ground. He rolled over and sat up. Dark volcanic rocks about the size of his fist made up the ground between him and the lake. Tall trees lined the edge of the small thirty metre semi circle he had landed in. His suit gave the exterior temperature as thirty seven degrees, humidity at one hundred and twenty two percent and a zero on the toxic elements in the ecosphere. He asked the suit to re run the toxic analysis, once again the result was zero. If this planet is so far removed from humanity there should be thousands of elements toxic to him, he assumed the suit was malfunctioning.

A communication from the other man's soul slammed into his mind with a startling force, Axel fell forwards and put his hands to his helmet. The same thought kept repeating in his mind, 'the lake, the lake'. Several large black bodies moved across the surface, Axel watched as the creatures emerged from the water and slip back down to disappear in the darkness. After crawling a few feet he reached the shoreline and peered into the odd gloom. Shades of colour momentarily flashed through the depths and illuminated the lake. Each bright fleeting glimpse revealed a countless number of creatures swimming through the mystifying lake. Just ahead of Axel, only a few feet into the water, the bottom dropped away beyond sight.

Axel rolled into the water and fell over the cliff edge. The suit lacked any buoyancy and he descended quickly. Occasional flashes of vibrant colour replaced the receding light of daytime above him. His body flinched as the creatures lightly bumped and knocked against him always pushing him toward the centre of the black void below. The other man's soul sent waves of elation and delight through Axel's mind. Axel however suffered only a feeling dread. A creature bumped it's nose into his face plate and he caught sight of some very menacing teeth. At the same time a wash pleasure saturated his already worried sensibility. He felt a grip on his ankle, a sudden pull on his leg tore his suit open and the cold water saturated his skin. Light pulses flashed brighter and the greater intensity left after images on his retina. He closed his eyes and tried to reverse his downward course but the suit weighed too much and his struggle came to nothing. Another creature ripped a hole in his suit across his torso and a further bite tore an opening out of the back. Within seconds several more creatures attacked in a frenzy and he was violently pulled and shoved in several directions in a swift attack. A blaze of vivid red light overwhelmed Axel and left him blinded in a haze of physical and mental anguish. With a flash of shocking force the other man's soul left his mind.

Axel awoke on the shore line of the massive lake. Despite all the violent attacks he had endured under the water he was relatively unhurt. His sore lungs laboured to pull in each breath but still he was able to relax, he found that the other man's soul was gone and at last he was free. The sound of the water lapping at his feet reminded him of his virtually fatal venture into the deep lake and he smiled with relief at his escape. An itch presented itself, he reached down and scratched his knee, there was no suit. Axel was on his feet in a second, the suit had disappeared and he stood naked on the shoreline. He quickly looked about the area but there was no sign of it, theoretically he should be dead from toxic shock but he remained seemingly perfectly healthy if a little bruised and tired. An odd sound from the lake called for his attention, an odd black bulge had emerged from the water and was moving to the shore. Each moment brought more confusion to Axel, he did not know what to expect when the soul was released to the water but the intense cry for freedom had driven Axel here and he had fulfilled the promise he had made to his comrade. He stumbled backwards away from the lake as the strange alien form came forward. The creature reached the shoreline and stopped apparently regarding him from a distance. Axel recognised the vaguely humanoid shape of the creature immediately, it was an enemy alien, a member of the Theast race that had been so comprehensively beaten they were considered

35

extinct. And yet one of them had come to Axel on this veiled planet and stood only a few feet away.

The alien was smaller than Axel but had more bulk about the body, two powerful arms reached down below the first pair of knees on its powerful double jointed legs. No facial sensory organs were apparent due to the mass of thick dark hair that totally covered the alien.

A telepathic link formed between them and Axel was able to make out the basic intention from the alien mind.

"Thank you."

What did that mean? Thank you? Axel remained as still as the alien but his body raced with adrenalin and fear.

"You bring me here. Me now die you."

Several questions chased through Axel's brain. Was he the other man's soul? Did I bring him here in the mistaken belief the soul was Gary's? Is he going to attack? Can I beat him in a fight? Is he faster than me? The questions ceased the moment the alien leapt forward. Axel turned and rushed up the rocky beach toward the pod, the lose rocks and his bare feet combined to slow his movement to a stumble. He fell onto his hands as he heard the alien land directly behind him. A powerful hand grasped his left shoulder and pulled him around. Axel grabbed a rock in his right hand and as he turned he used the momentum to beat the alien across its face. The grip on him weakened and he turned once more to run for the pod.

The alien let out a piercing, terrifying scream sending a cold wave of fear across Axel's entire body.

"My people all die, you guilty, you die."

Axel stopped to face his enemy, he could not allow himself to be attacked from behind again. He had been lucky to have struck the first blow but the alien would not be so easy next time. The weight of the rocks in each of his hands gave him little assurance. He watched the alien move gradually forward with great anxiety. It moved to the side and he realised it wanted to get between him and the pod. As he took his first step the alien attacked using it's muscular legs to advance at a startling speed, Axel brought up both of his hands and tried to catch the alien's head between the two rocks. He failed to bring home the attack as intended but caught the side of the foul smelling dark head with a glancing blow. A spray of blood spewed over Axel's face when he fell backwards with the alien on top of him. He dropped the rocks and managed take hold of one of the alien's arms as he was struck across the face. He fumbled to grab the alien's other hand but failed and received another blow directly on his nose. Pain shot through his skull as the blood from the injury trickled into the back of his throat. Again he was struck on the nose, his eyes closed in a chaos of movement and tearful agony. Their hands moved quickly trying to find a way through the struggle to inflict pain and damage on each other. He tried to push the creature off and found it easier than he expected. Axel rolled away from the alien and picked up another rock as he moved. His enemy jumped high in a trajectory that would have brought precisely on top of Axel but he moved just in time and the alien landed wrong footed and fell on his front. Axel seized the creature's head by the hair and brought the rock down on it in a powerful strike.

Axel fell on to his backside and dropped the rock. The alien lay still either dead or unconscious. He felt a sudden tremendous guilt weigh upon him, this alien was the last of his species and even though it had been a fight for his survival Axel wished he had not struck the creature so hard. Blood seeped from the wound Axel had so easily inflicted in his blind attack. "My god. What have I done?" He said.

Axel turned the exterior handle and opened the pod door. He stepped on the one rung and reached inside through the tiny hatch into the locker to look for a medical kit. The mess and bulk of Captain Balucci's suit caused him to lean in further and rummage through the clutter without looking. His hand came upon a cold metallic object, he pulled it out and found a plasma gun in his hand. He glanced back to view the alien creature only to find it missing, no sound had caught his ear, the alien must have moved very quietly. Axel gripped the gun tightly as he surveyed the area around him. There was a rustling sound behind and he turned too late, a crushing blow sent him reeling onto the rocks, the gun skittered away from his hand. The alien moved to sit on Axel and deliver another attack, Axel kicked up at the creature and struck him in the centre of the chest. Axel rolled over and crawled to the gun, he picked it up, turned and aimed it at his adversary. The alien jumped and landed with each foot on either side of his torso, it raised its hand in preparation to bring the rock down on his head. Axel found it impossible to fire, he could not be responsible for killing this creature and bringing about the extinction of its race. He dropped the gun and allowed the rock to be brought down on his skull.

JACK STONE

Jack Stone waited patiently in line, his calm exterior betrayed none of his inner fear. He thought he would never leave Earth again, that there would be no reason good enough to risk returning to prison but that was before Eric's call. The line moved forward, Jack checked the time on his watch and put his hand in the pocket containing his fake passport.

Two weeks ago he had been released from a three year prison term for attempting to smuggle alien fauna onto Earth. His elation after his release had soon fizzled out. The lodgings the prison board had secured for him were little better than his cell and his hopes of finding a job had quickly collapsed. A dark mood had settled upon him, he found something to criticise or complain about everywhere he looked. He would return to prison if he was caught trying to leave but Eric's passion for his discovery had been intense. He said he had found something truly amazing, something that would change their lives forever.

The line moved forward, Jack pulled his false passport from his pocket and pushed his bag forward with his foot. The passenger ahead of Jack finished checking in and he stepped forward to the desk. He caught the girl's eyes and smiled as he handed over his documents. Her heavily applied lipstick fought to gain his attention from her extraordinary eye makeup. Jack wondered if he could actually see any of her skin or if it was all hidden under her standard issue face cake. He received his passport back with a boarding pass, walked through the gate and up the ramp.

The shuttle lifted him into orbit with little fuss and Jack soon remembered how much he enjoyed space travel. The transfer to the Bloxmore corporation interstellar ferry took little time and he was soon directed to his stasis pod. He lay back in the coffin like bed and imagined how terrible it might be to wake up mid journey and be unable to release the lid. A standard issue face cake was the last thing he saw as the top of the pod closed over him.

It was opened an instant or three weeks later, depending on your viewpoint, by a young lady with no face cake whatsoever. "Hello Sir, welcome to Bloxmore." She said.

"Thank you." Jack replied. After three weeks sleep he hoped he may have felt a great sense of peace and relaxation but all he had was an aching back. The sign over the arrivals gate said 'Welcome to Bloxmore'. "Well Eric, you better have something here." he muttered under his breath.

Eric Black waited at the arrival gate looking so healthy it would be considered rude. "Let me take your bag Jack I've got a trolley here, it insists on going sideways but I'm sure we can get it to the car."

Jack offered his hand but was surprised when Eric leant forward and hugged him. It had been over three years since they were last together and Jack wouldn't like to admit it but he was very happy to see his old friend. The deeply imbedded depression Jack carried with him lifted a little and brought a sorrowful, longing smile to his face.

Eric struggled with the trolley all the way to his red Ford Bloxmore and dumped the bag on the back seat. His excitement in meeting his old friend had Eric giggling and darting about in a most exasperating manner. Jack helped himself to the passenger seat and waited until they were out of the car park and onto the dirt road before asking about Eric's discovery. "So, what the bloody hell am I doing here?"

Eric grinned and drummed his fingers on the steering wheel. He looked at Jack and spoke slowly spacing the words for more dramatic impact. "I was out exploring the foothills close to my village and I found a large hole in the rock face. On closer inspection I realised it was not a natural opening." He stopped talking and pulled the car to the side of the road. With his eyes open wide he continued the story. "It was built by aliens. A large room inside the hill contained nothing but a small extraterrestrial device."

Jack put his head in his hands. "Oh bloody hell, just turn the car around and take me back to the airport."

Eric talked quickly hoping to rescue the situation. "No, no it's true, mankind has finally found proof of intelligent alien life."

"You've finally gone mad." Jack spoke with no levity, he was annoyed and disappointed. All his savings wasted on this fool's errand. He thought Eric had found some mineral on his land that would make them rich not a so called bloody alien device.

Eric put his hand on Jack's forearm and tried to reason with him. "Come to my house and see it, just look at it. I promise you will not be disappointed."

Jack sat in the car facing forwards and said nothing.

Eric started the engine and set off once again down the dirt road. Jack remained silent for the entire ride.

The village of Wivelsfield had been placed in a valley thirty miles north of the spaceport. The design of the buildings harked back to a romantic Victorian England and Jack tutted at the sickly sweet counterfeit ambience.

Eric parked the car in front of his large house and lifted Jack's bag from the back seat.

Jack followed Eric into his home. The lavish surroundings surprised him and he took his time looking around at the handsome interior. "Well this is nice, how did you manage this?" Jack asked.

"I was in sewage." Eric replied.

"You were in what?" Jack laughed as he spoke.

Eric continued, ignoring Jack's laughter. "You know when I left school my first job was in sewage management. Well I fooled them into thinking that was my expertise. I worked in sewage for ten years setting up the system in the city." Eric disappeared into the kitchen and returned a few moments later with an old wooden box. He put it proudly on the table and stood back. "Well here it is."

Jack looked at the box, back at Eric, back at the box and then commented. "Very impressive."

With a look to the heavens Eric stepped forwards and opened the box. He reached in and lifted out a metallic cube four inches to a side. Its surface was completely free of markings.

Jack commented again. "Equally impressive."

Eric picked up the cube and with a loud clap disappeared into thin air.

Jack sat still for a moment trying to come to grips with what he had just witnessed. As his mind couldn't make sense of this occurrence he waited in a stunned silence. Every passing second seemed as an hour as Eric delayed his reappearance. Finally his heart leapt when the thundering silence was shattered by Eric's sudden laughter from the Kitchen. Jack could only find two words. "Bloody hell."

Eric emerged smiling broadly. Without taking his eyes off Jack he found a chair and sat holding the precious cube in front of him. Finally Eric realised it was he who had to break the silence. "It's a teleportation device. Do you want to try it?"

Jack slowly raised his hand and waved away the offer. A ripple of sparkling energy caressed the fine nerves of his frame sending a cold wave of sensation across his body. A self satisfied Eric reclined gleefully opposite Jack's shocked psyche. With none of his previous practised sullen demeanour Jack spoke, humbled. "Why me? Why did you ask me here? What can I do? What do you want from me?"

Eric sat forward and replied with an intense gaze. "I had to ask you here, you are the only person I can trust."

Jack was confused. "Trust? What can I do?"

Eric placed the cube back in the box and sat down. "I want to take it to Earth before I tell anyone about it." Eric said.

Jack was now a little calmer and decided to ask some pertinent questions. "Take it to Earth? But why? If you take this to the Bloxmore head office you'll go down in history, not to mention the money you'll make."

Eric shook his head, leaned forwards and whispered in Jack's ear. "I don't trust them. Bloxmore will want this for themselves and anyway when you sign up for a place on a corporate colony you sign over all your rights. Anything of any value you find on the colony planet is automatically owned by the corporation, its' in the contract."

Jack took a brief moment for contemplation before continuing his cross-examination. "OK, say for a moment you could get it onto Earth. Then what?" Jack asked.

"I hand it over to a news group and claim I found it with you. Coffee?" Eric entered the kitchen leaving his friend to think.

Jack picked the cube out of the box and examined it. "It is certainly well sealed." He said "How did you find out it was a teleportation device?"

Eric shouted his reply from the kitchen. "When I first picked it up it was very dirty and I just thought it would be easier to see what it was if I was outside. An instant later there I was."

Jack put the cube on the table and talked as he collected his coffee from the kitchen. "If you take this to Earth it could be very dangerous. We don't know what powers the thing. It could be giving us a huge dose of radiation as we speak. What if it is powered by anti matter and somebody tries to open it?"

Eric became quite animated in his reply. "But you don't know any of that to be true. You are just making up nonsense."

"You still haven't said why me. Why do you want my help?" Jack asked.

"You are the only smuggler I know."

Despite Eric's serious tone Jack laughed. "You mean I am the only failed smuggler you know. I tried to smuggle alien flowers onto Earth and they caught me, if you think that qualifies me for your plan then you have some serious thinking to do. Why don't you just teleport yourself to Earth?"

Eric shook his head. "I don't want to risk it. Teleporting down the road or into another room is OK but across a few light years? I'll leave that to someone else."

Jack and Eric sat opposite each other in silence as they finished their coffee. Jack was torn inside, his life had been going downhill at a depressing pace back on Earth and now something extraordinary had appeared. It was exciting and it made him feel alive again. So why was he looking for excuses to duck out of it?

Eric picked up the cube and placed it back in the box.

Finally Jack asked a question. "How does it work?"

"Well you've just been in the kitchen. Imagine the space and just think you want to be there."

Jack picked up the cube and held it in front of his face. He disappeared from the room and instantly reappeared in the kitchen. Finding himself teleported electrified his mood and he yelped spontaneously. On entering the living room he found Eric sitting opposite the door, his smile beaming.

After dinner Jack had made up his mind to help. Eric's startling find had brought a feeling to Jack he hadn't felt for many years and his initial fear had transformed into enthusiasm. They had come up with a plan to get the cube through Bloxmore security and then Earth customs. Smuggling something nobody was looking for should be very easy, if no one is looking for it, then why hide it? It was this strategy Eric and Jack adopted. Jack would carry the cube in his bag and if asked, it was a present for someone back on Earth.

43

The day of the trip arrived and both Jack and Eric awoke before their alarm clocks sprang to life. The journey to the spaceport in the red Ford Bloxmore was uneventful and somehow reassuring. Not a word was said as they approached the town.

Eric left the vehicle in the long term car park and threw the keys into a bin as they came close to the spaceport.

Jack's heart rate soared as he entered the building he paused and gazed up at the sign, 'Welcome to Bloxmore'. He looked at Eric and smiled. "Well time to do it, let's have some fun shall we." He walked off purposefully towards the check in desk.

Eric followed with a more cautious stride attempting a relaxed nonchalance.

Jack looked the girl in the eye and smiled as he spoke. "Hello, how are you?" He handed over his return ticket and passport.

He was seized by a sudden shocking dizziness, his perception spiralled and as he collapsed he could only close his eyes to block out this traumatic twisting reality. And at once his distress ceased. Through his drowsiness he became aware of his immediate environment, he was lying naked on some sort of bed. He opened his eyes but quickly closed them to shut out the painful glare. To his left he heard a vaguely familiar voice.

"He is awake now, turn down the lighting."

The light dimmed sufficiently for him to open his eyes. He took in his surroundings with complete disbelief. He was back in prison, lying on some sort of surgical bed with wires attached to every limb and several to his skull. To his right technicians adjusted several pieces of equipment and to his left, through a window, he could see several men in suits, they stood up and made their way out of the room. Jack's extreme shock at finding himself back in prison was matched only by his sadness. He was barely able to move, one of the technicians commented that the paralysis would wear off quite quickly. He could not find a reason to want the paralysis to wear off.

The cables were removed from his body, he was dressed in a surgical smock, transferred to a trolley and wheeled into the recovery room. Four of the men in suits entered with Jack's lawyer and the prison's deputy warden. Jack was still struggling to make sense of what was happening as he listened to the deputy warden speak.

44

"Jack Stone, you have failed the parole release simulation. When given the opportunity to break the law you did so and you are therefore denied release at this time. You will be eligible for parole again in one year."

Jack's lawyer remained in the room as the officials left, he talked quietly and patted Jack's shoulder. "Sorry Jack, you know they run these simulations, you should have been more careful."

The cell was just as he left it. The guards let him walk in and then locked the cage door behind him. He stood in the centre of the small cubicle staring at the wall ahead of him. The simulation had been perfect, he could not have known he was existing in an imitation world, a bogus universe where every thought, every move he made was being watched and recorded. He lay on his bunk and turned to face the wall, another year of this way of life was beyond contemplation. Waves of cold anguish washed over him, the core of his being empty and without purpose. He lay on his side staring at the wall for what seemed an eternity.

'Clap'. The sound was not so much familiar as alarming, Jack stared at the wall. He heard the sound of somebody's footwear shift on the concrete floor. Then the voice, a voice he should not have heard. It was Eric.

"Jack, quickly, before they spot me, hold onto the other side and we'll get out of here."

Jack rolled over to see Eric anxiously holding out the metallic cube. He struggled to come to terms with this turn of events, the Eric standing in his cell, talking to him must be a rogue fantasy figure, some sort of leftover hope from the simulation.

Eric looked over his shoulder to see if he had been detected, Jack merely watched with little real interest. He viewed this incarnation in his cell as he would a hologram, a totally artificial construct, something he was, of course, unable to interact with. The cell block alarm screamed its distress to the guards as the red warning light flashed over the door of Jack's cell.

Eric moved to the cell cage door and checked the area. Four prison guards appeared from the far door at the end of the cell block and broke into a sprint.

Jack sat forward on his bunk completely perplexed. How could this illusion have set off the alarm? He watched Eric's hand move over to his shoulder and felt him pull at his clothing, the

45

guards reached the cell and hesitated a moment as they caught sight of the intruder. The cell door opened as Jack touched the cube and disappeared into thin air.

Darkness and silence greeted Jack the instant after had he teleported out of the prison cell. He was lying on his back shocked, saddened, confused and apprehensive. To move an arm would be to discover his current predicament, a predicament he might just as well prefer to remain unknown. But of course there was no alternative he could not lie unmoving forever. His breath informed him he was in a very small space perhaps coffin sized but far too comfortable to be a resting place of the deceased. It was then the location became apparent, he was in a stasis pod. He raised his arms and thankfully the lid opened without protest. He sat up and viewed his surroundings with suspicion. Hundreds of pods, lined up in rows, took up most of the floor space in this large bay. The pod he sat in was possibly the actual one he had travelled to Bloxmore in but there were so many it was difficult to tell. Apart from the dull hum of the ships' systems he was in a silent environment. There was no sign of activity from the crew, he thought perhaps that a passenger waking in mid flight would have set off some sort of an alarm but so far there was no reaction at all.

Jack made his way to the bay door and activated the lock. The next bay was exactly the same, rows and rows of pods and no activity. He stood for a moment in the doorway and looked back and forth between the two bays, it was then he noticed the computer terminal built into the wall. The screensaver Bloxmore logo bounced and twisted slowly in the display, he pressed a couple of keys but there was no response. After surveying the scene for a few more moments he made his way to the nearest pod, the display indicated it was empty and so was the next, empty. Empty, empty, empty, there was not one other passenger. Where could a starship be going with no people? A dark confusion slightly tainted with fear tugged at his peripheral emotions. He decided he must find the bridge and speak to the crew, his eyes darted around the bay looking for a doorway that may lead elsewhere away from the pod bays. Nothing was immediately apparent and he decided to enter the next bay and then the next but still no exit presented itself. Breathless and desperate he stopped at the door to another bay and pressed the release tab, the door opened to reveal an identical bay to the last. Just as he was setting off to the next door he glanced over his shoulder and caught sight of a man disappearing into the bay he had just left. Jack shouted a hello, his voice echoed in the enormous space but there was no reply. He ran to the doorway and found the man was without substance, a fleeting glimpse brought about by a desperate mind. After a few steps backwards Jack found the wall and slipped down it to rest, seated but uncomfortable. He looked up at the ceiling and rested the back of his head on the wall, a very slight sound called for his attention. Looking forwards again he could see between the wall and the first row of pods, directly ahead of him and only partly in view, was a door.

As Jack approached it opened, he stopped and peered through. The corridor beyond curved to the left out of sight, Jack shouted hello but again received no reply. Now more worried and cautious than desperate, Jack slowly moved down the passageway. It terminated at a small lobby, opposite him were three doors, each with a sign above, Engineering, Bridge and Personnel. Jack decided on the Bridge, stepped forwards to the door and pressed the button. The door slid open to reveal a lift, he stepped in and was carried upwards. The door opened, standing in the centre of the bridge was Eric. "Eric where are we? What have you done?"

Eric took a step forwards and opened his mouth, his lips shaped the words but no sound came.

Jack neared him and closer inspection revealed Eric was not actually on the bridge but an odd hologramatic image.

Eric tried to communicate again, his frustration obvious by the strained, almost tearful, expression. "We have bounced into alternative realities."

The words now clear did nothing to clarify Jack's situation. "They have shown me the way free of this confinement, you must do as I say." Eric said.

"Bloody alien artefact!" Jack muttered.

Eric's image fluttered and he looked to his left as if appealing to someone or something out of sight. "Return to the pod where you awoke. Close the lid and think of yourself back on Bloxmore with me."

Finding the original pod was easy as he had left the lid open. The coffin like dimensions stirred his slight claustrophobia and stimulated his morbid imagination.

Eric's hologram smiled as Jack stepped into the pod. The lid closed with a soft bump, complete darkness did nothing to help his current nervous temperament. He closed his eyes and imagined the kitchen at Eric's house on Bloxmore just as he had when he first teleported. 'Clap'. Light was immediately apparent through his eyelids, the smell of fresh coffee slowed his heart and on opening his eyes the sight of Eric smiling hastened it. "Am I here? Is this normality?"

Eric nodded and put his arms around Jack. The cube lifted from the table and with a loud clap disappeared.

THE LAST ASTRONAUT

Toby Lincoln took one final breath and disconnected the oxygen supply between his suit and the land car. He pulled the toggle to open the exterior airlock door and gripped the side handles ready to propel himself forward. If he was fast enough he would make it to the base in time and be inside quickly. If he was too slow he would suffer a rather undignified, futile death. There was no choice, his back-up tanks were empty and the land car's scrubbers were no longer functioning. If he stayed put he would die.
The door opened too slowly and he focussed his mind in an effort to control his frustration, he looked down at the mottled gravel that made up the ground between him and the base and recalled how eager he had been to step out of the airlock the first day they had arrived. The door stopped halfway, he grabbed it with both hands and slowly pushed it aside. At last there was enough space and he pulled himself out of the land car and onto the Martian surface. Just twenty yards and he can enter the base. He prayed not all the systems had crashed, they shouldn't have, the base was heavily shielded against radiation but still he had doubts. The land car had suffered minor damage if only because it was such a basic, rugged design. The airlock didn't respond. Toby opened the emergency flap to his side and twisted the manual release. The handle resisted his attempts at movement and turned with a slow, stiff rotation. The deteriorating gas mix in his suit was taking its toll, a slight dizziness tainted his perception and brought on an intense headache. Finally the airlock door opened enough for him to enter and he fell inwards. He pulled the emergency air supply tube from its recess and connected it to his suit. Intermittent blasts of carbon dioxide discharged from the exit valve on the back of his helmet as the clean air filtered into the suit's atmosphere compressor. His dizziness cleared slowly and he remained on his back waiting for the pain to subside.
His return journey to the base had been both shocking and desperate. Radio communication had ceased as soon as the radiation had hit his land car but he couldn't tell if it was a failure of his equipment or they were simply not responding. If all the crew had died he would bury them alone and say a few words, something he had never been good at but he would do his best. He realised he was

coming close to weeping and coughed to try and stifle his emotional outburst. Tears blurred his vision and he blinked the liquid out of his eyes.

After what seemed like an hour he got to his feet and closed the exterior airlock door. He ran the decontamination system and expelled the atmosphere from within the small compartment. A standard human friendly gaseous mix filled the space and he was free to enter the base. Toby strained with the effort of forcing the interior door to one side, he muttered obscenities as he slid into the gap and pushed the door further open with his knee. His suit lights cast two powerful beams into the dark corridor. Thankfully there was no sign of damage, the land car's lights had blown out immediately and scattered small particles of glass across its cabin. If the same thing had happened here there should have been debris everywhere but it was clean. Environment filters in his suit indicated an uncontaminated atmosphere. He unlocked the catches on his helmet and lifted it off. "Hello. Gary? Bill? Michelle? Is there anybody here?" Toby's call was met with silence.

He continued through the base and made his way to the reactors. The emergency trip switches had all triggered. After he had flipped them all back to the open position the lighting came to life and the base wide systems started up automatically. None of the reactor's control structure could be engaged without a thorough overhaul and the base was left with battery power only.

Toby switched the intercom to general call. His voice was amplified through every speaker in the base but still he received no reply.

In the mission room each of the crew's environment suits were in their lockers, they could not have left the base without them and yet the crew were missing. Toby removed his suit and changed into his base uniform. Nasty images flowed through his mind as he worried about finding his crewmate's bodies in various states of mutilation.

The command centre was empty. Toby sat himself at the science station and searched the entire base through the closed circuit cameras, he found not a single person or any signs of a hurried exit. The second land car was parked exactly where it should be. The communications array was in good order but neither the Earth uplink or the distress beacon were activated. He moved to the

51

medical station and brought up the crew location screen. The medical monitor implants were permanently connected to the system via a triple back up microwave link and yet he could not locate a single crewmember. The range was over three miles and the fact not a single icon appeared on the screen sent a chill down his spine. Next he moved to the communications station, activated the transmission beacon and lined up a tight beam on Earth's mission control satellite.

"This is an emergency priority one message. All crew missing but myself. We have suffered an intense gamma ray burst. The base is now operating on backup power only. Land car one damaged, condition of land car two unknown. Life support and other class one systems working at optimum. Please advise on next course of action." He headed back to his locker, put on his suit and connected a new oxygen tank.

Land car two appeared perfectly normal as he approached, another puzzle for his already taxed mind. The airlock functioned perfectly and he climbed in. To Toby's relief the apparatus powered up normally, he put the car into drive and accelerated in the direction of the escape rocket.

As the journey progressed his mind turned once more to his crewmates and his worries for their well being. And yet there were no bodies, no evidence of suffering or even an indication they were in the base at the time of the radioactive assault. He punched the console in frustration and uttered an excess of swear words.

He decelerated as he passed over a rocky outcrop and got his first view of the escape rocket. It stood on its launch pad embraced by a large support frame as if located in the ribcage of a long dead enormous steel beast. He made his way to the cockpit and started the long systems checklist.

A low repetitive buzzing alarm indicated a communication had been received from ground control. Toby leaned over and activated the message packet.

"This is Jack Stone, we are very pleased to hear from you Toby. The loss of contact after the aggressive event had us all extremely worried. I'm afraid that your suggestion this was a gamma ray burst was incorrect. We detected a very powerful beam of energy originating from within the asteroid belt. As the beam was only one hundred miles in diameter we can only assume it was not a natural phenomenon. The Earth uplink was put out of action by the energy beam. Can you re-start the encryption computers for us? We will check all of the base's systems from here. Can you clarify your statement that all the crew are missing? We are working up an exit strategy to get you off the planet and back here as soon as possible. We will send another message when we are ready. Please begin to prep the escape rocket now."

Not a natural phenomenon? What did that mean? Toby turned on the transmission beacon. "Hello Jack, message received. Escape rocket is now being prepared for launch. I have been unable to locate any members of the crew or their bodies by any means. Medical monitors are not responding and their environment suits are still in their lockers. Can you clarify your statement that the beam was not natural?" He flicked off the beacon and returned to the rocket's preparation. A red icon caught his attention on the oxygen reserve; the supply was down to ten percent. The radiation beam must have damaged the oxygen storage assembly in the rocket's support bunker. He would have to bring several large tanks over from the base and that could take all day. The land car was built to carry two people and a small amount of equipment on a weak cargo frame. The oxygen tanks were very heavy he and didn't know if the frame could handle more than one at a time.

The communication alarm buzzed, a new message had arrived but it couldn't be a reply. The time it takes for a message to get to Earth and then an answer to be sent back is just too long, this must be something else.

Jack Stone sounded quite perturbed. "Okay Toby, now we've got some disturbing news. We traced the beam back to its origin as near as we could and it appears there is something out there between Mars and the Asteroid Belt. We have triple checked and there is no mistake. Hubble three is still functioning around the Moon so we are going to try and turn it around and get a picture of what's out there. I will contact you as soon as anything new is learned on the anomaly."

Anomaly? Now that was a typical Jack Stone understatement.

The storage building was connected to the main base by a long pressurised walkway. He parked as close to the main airlock as he could and exited the land car.

As he entered the storeroom he faced several empty oxygen tanks lined up on a large rack opposite the door. He pulled one off the wall and stumbled backwards as he struggled to hold it upright, the weight was difficult to handle even in Mars' weak gravity. He fumbled with a trolley and managed to secure the tank to its frame. One of the trolley wheels squealed under the strain of containing the weight as Toby pushed it to the airlock through which he had entered. After transporting it out to the land car he rested it against the door while he released the straps on the cargo frame. The first strap was secured to the top of the tank and Toby lifted it by the bottom and struggled to swing it up and onto the support. He felt a sudden powerful stinging in his right knee as the tank slipped into position. Flashes of sharp lightning fast pain shot up his leg as he stumbled to the land car airlock. He pulled himself in and massaged his injury as he waited for the pain to recede. Irritation surfaced for the first time since the energy beam hit the base. If he couldn't move the oxygen to the escape rocket he was stranded. The first land car was beyond use, the tanks were too heavy and now his knee was injured. He took an emergency painkiller out of the medical pack, opened the sachet and swallowed the awful liquid. A quick angry jab at the control panel switched the car into drive and he headed out to the rocket's launch site steering with one hand on the wheel and the other on his knee.

Oxygen flowed slowly through from the tank to the escape rocket's reservoir. Toby turned away and looked into the sky, the setting sun cast a long shadow in front of him and he looked down in a moment of introspection as the tank emptied its contents. The oxygen gauge in the cockpit registered an extra seven percent. Seventy percent was the minimum level required, he would need another nine tanks to reach that level but he was sure he would not be able to lift another. If he travelled back and forth with enough of the small personnel tanks he could increase the quantity to the required level but it would take days. There had to be another way. The communications beacon buzzed again, Toby accessed the message.

"Hello Toby. Hubble Three has given us a fuzzy image of what can only be a vessel of some kind. Doppler shift indicates that the craft is decelerating from a tremendous speed. It is currently on course for Mars and will be with you in less than twenty-four hours. You can boost into orbit and rendezvous with the orbital in two hours otherwise you will have wait for it to come around again."

Jack Stone's timbre changed to a quieter more worried tone. "We have done a detailed search of the base and the surrounding area through the uplink and we can find no trace of the other crew members. We know you are on your own there Toby. We wish you the best of luck."

He flicked the message off and put his head in his hands. "Not enough time, not enough time." He mumbled. He told himself to think imaginatively. The large tanks were too heavy, the personnel tanks were too small and there was not enough oxygen in the rocket to carry him into orbit. Two hours. If he counted in the start up for the rocket it was even less. Realistically he had the time for one more trip to the base. He clambered into the land car and made his way back, the empty tank was still on the cargo frame and he could use that if he could work out a way to fill it without taking it off the land car.

As soon as he had parked he scrambled out of the land car and into the airlock, the oxygen supply hose snaked out of its recess as he pulled it out to see how long it was. Three feet at best. It reached just outside the door. Even the oxygen hose that connected his personnel tank to his helmet wouldn't help. He had a sudden flash of inspiration and activated the airlock sequence. It could not cycle fast enough for him. The internal door opened, he charged out of it, ran through to the crew suit lockers, collected up all the personnel hoses he could find and returned to the airlock. After he had attached the first tube to the oxygen valve he connected the others together in chain and linked the final one to the large tank on the land car. The gas slowly passed through and Toby took the opportunity to collect the rest of the personnel tanks. With the cabin full of as many small tanks as he could fit he disconnected the hose and closed the airlock.

The contents of the large tank discharged into the rocket's reservoir as Toby put the personnel tanks by the maintenance hatch. Oxygen was at twenty four percent, enough to get off Mars but not enough to chase the orbital if he blasted off too late.

A buzzing alerted him to another message. "Hello Toby I have some bad news. The alien has stopped decelerating is at a constant speed that will bring it to you much sooner than we thought. It may enter orbit while you are still there. We cannot bring the schedule forward as the orbital will not be in position. We have

55

programmed the escape rocket via the uplink for a quick rendezvous with the orbital. We will keep you updated."

Toby flicked on the transmitter. "Message received. I am preparing to boost into orbit in twenty minutes as planned. Oxygen level now at twenty four percent but I do have eighteen personnel tanks to discharge into the system." He switched off the communications array and jumped out of the hatch. A powerful stinging shock reminded him of his injured knee and he hobbled to a stop by the maintenance hatch. Each personnel tank could be connected to the main reservoir through both the maintenance hatch and the main valve. Toby busied himself linking each small tank in turn at the two connections. Several of the tanks contained less than he had hoped but the oxygen level increased at a constant rate.

An alarm sounded in the cockpit, Toby quickly pulled himself up the ladder and switched on the communications display. The geo-stationary satellite over the base had spotted the incoming alien craft. It had reached Mars earlier than he had expected. Video from the satellite revealed an ominous black shape moving slowly across the star field. Size and shape was impossible to guess at with the low-resolution cameras on the satellite providing little detail.

Cold unfamiliar waves of sensation washed over his frame and propelled him into a state of fear. The alien craft that quite probably had killed his three companions was now overhead. Toby pulled himself out of the cockpit in a frantic rush and raced down the frame to the ground level. He disconnected the empty oxygen tanks, he couldn't wait any longer, there would just have to be enough.

Satellite tracking indicated the orbital moving through its normal path to the rendezvous position. Final procedures came online as Toby started working through the pre-launch start up. Green icons lit up across his display with only the oxygen level showing an amber light. The rocket sealed itself and discharged the ground support cables. Toby had to lean over the co-pilot seat to initiate all the launch events but once he had completed the crew side of the process all he could do was sit back and wait impatiently for the computer to fire the engines and lift him into orbit.

He fixed his eyes on the dark shape taking up half of the video screen. There were no lights visible, which could mean they have no windows, which could mean they have no eyes. He realised this kind of analysis would get him nowhere. A large red light in the corner of the cockpit flashed three times and all the icons on his display blinked red to indicate lift off in ten seconds. Locking clamps released the rocket from the launch pad and Toby felt his body weight increase as the main engines lifted the small vessel off the ground. The craft accelerated at such a speed it seemed to Toby it had leapt off the surface of the planet. Gee forces increased steadily as the rocket gained height, the noise level in the cockpit reached an ear damaging level and he realised he had forgotten to put on his suit helmet.

Toby lifted off his seat as he reached orbit. A loud bang followed by a noisy mechanical clunk resonated through the cockpit as the main rocket section was discarded. Small jets of gas fired out of the tiny stabilising motors ringing the circumference of the lonely crew section. He craned his neck trying to see the alien craft through the small window. His heart stumbled as he caught sight of the enormous black vessel. It filled half of the sky as a dark eternal mass sucking in the light of the galaxy and stubbornly refusing to release a single photon. The orbital came into view below the vast alien ship moving slowly in its own ponderous arc. Toby set up a laser link and synchronised computers for emergency docking. Thrusters fired and he suffered a moment of dizziness as the as the tiny gee forces harassed his directional perception.

A beam of intense white light connected the alien ship with the orbital and snapped off in an instant. Toby watched opened mouthed as he waited for the inevitable explosion, time passed and nothing happened. He tightened his straps and secured himself back into his seat. The orbital reached the close docking position and fired small thrusters to properly align itself with the crew section. Toby switched off the autopilot and took control of the vehicle. He targeted the laser range finder on the approaching location mirror set in the side of the orbital. Small directional thrusters blew tiny streams of gas away in a rapid sequence as his small crew section closed on its astral partner. The two vehicles bumped together and Toby activated the docking clamps. Four tiny arms reached out seized the waiting restraint rings and pulled the umbilical across to link with the airlock.

Toby moved out of his seat and opened the interior door. He put on his helmet, sealed his suit and attached a guide rope to a crew ring. The door closed behind him and the passageway pressurised, he crossed the umbilical and cycled through into the orbital. His suit registered with the main computer and received an all safe on the life support systems.

After reaching the bridge he set up the laser communications link with Earth and sent a quick message. "This Toby Lincoln on board the Mars orbital. The alien ship has entered an identical orbit but has made no effort to communicate. It seems it has probed the orbital in some way but there are no apparent signs of damage. I will be exiting Mars orbit as scheduled in thirty five minutes."

A series of intense beams of light shifting in colour and width reached across from the alien ship and connected to the orbital. Occasional bright shafts of light stabbed through the window and left a lasting image on Toby's retina. Ship wide systems spasmed as the alien sensors penetrated every part of the small human craft. The lighting flashed rapidly forcing a strobed perception of the interior and the atmosphere alarm sounded until choking off. A sudden moment of silence and complete darkness was replaced by a disturbing normality. Toby waited for another barrage but nothing came and he relaxed a little. He quickly set up an internal diagnostic and examined the life support systems himself. The three other crewmembers medical monitors registered on the display, he checked their location. The software placed them a little over one mile off the orbital. He peered through the window at the dark alien craft.

Laser light from the range finder bounced off the hull of the massive ship, the mysterious silhouette reflected less than ten percent of the original luminance but it registered a distance of one mile.

The satellite dish on the orbital lined up on Earth and Toby recorded his message. "I have located the medical monitors for the rest of the crew on board the alien ship..."

Light flooded his vision and he suffered a sudden intense headache. The brightness winked off and Toby realised he was lying on his back on a cold hard floor, through his eyelids he became aware of light and he opened his eyes. He looked around and found himself in an empty room. Each of the curved walls surrounding him emitted a red glow colouring the room in a shade he knew well as the Martian norm.

A quiet rumbling sound resonated throughout the room with no definable source, it lacked any intelligible meaning but Toby had the impression of an attempt at communication. It ceased abruptly. He rolled onto his front and looked around the room. No door, no furniture and the walls lacked any texture as if made purely from light. Once again the rumbling disjointed noise resounded about him, it modulated and distorted until it resembled a human voice. Syllables and consonants became apparent but still lacked any sense of meaning. Toby twisted up into a cross-legged position and put his hands over his ears; he hoped this gesture would indicate a lack of understanding. The noise stopped, he breathed a sigh of relief, the volume was not helping his headache.

A series of thoughts brushed his mind, light feelings of comprehension so soft he might have ignored them but they felt so alien. The essence of another intelligence, wholly extraordinary and foreign suddenly penetrated his psyche. Toby was rendered completely helpless as the aggressive presence rummaged through his mind. Memories, thoughts, feelings and sensory experience were all exposed and studied until without warning the examination stopped.

"Toby Lincoln?" The voice was his own.

"Yes?" He couldn't think of anything else to say.

"You are to be the witness."

A cascade of terrible violent imagery assaulted his mind. The sight of his crewmates' bodies, torn to pieces in a violent and merciless death, pounded on his awareness. "What have you done?" He cried. His heart rate leapt, the fear of his own imminent death and the shock of losing his friends in such a terrible way wounded him physically as well as emotionally. He lunged forward and vomited. The choking spasm worried him little as the basic natural fear of dying caused all of his muscles to quiver violently. He finished emptying his stomach and fell forward into the mess of juices. He curled up and hugged himself as his stomach continued to contract and expand the vomit reflex.

The alien presence washed through his mind. "You have no need to fear, we wish you no harm." The voice said.

Toby found little consolation in the statement but his body relaxed a little. "Why did you kill them?" He asked.

"Their deaths are a warning. You are the witness. We will not let your vile species free again."

"I don't understand. Free from where? From what?" Toby's mind was taken away from the room and he found himself as if floating in space over a beautiful planet, as rich in life and colour as Earth. But clearly not Earth, clearly an alien planet and Toby knew somehow it was home to humanity. The original home from where the first humans reached out into space. His sight was drawn away to a vessel high up above the North Pole travelling at a tremendous speed. The craft changed course and revealed behind it a massive asteroid it had towed to such a high velocity. The rock struck the planet like a bullet through an apple and shattered the crust in an explosion of cosmic energy. Toby reeled at the shock of the sight before him and instantly it was gone and silence and darkness held him alone.

"We reduced your original planet to a field of asteroids and allowed a few thousand of your ancestors to thrive on the fourth planet. But they too ventured too far into space. It was deemed necessary to remove a small number to the third planet before executing the ecosystem on the world you call Mars."
As the voice continued the tale Toby witnessed a similar asteroid impact on Mars but with far less power, reducing the globe to a barren lifeless rock.

"With no memory of your aggressive criminal past it was hoped humanity would evolve into a mature peaceful race. It was not to be. We have watched, sorrowful and desperate as you fight amongst yourselves and commit the most disgusting atrocities on each other. You will not be permitted to leave your planet and bleed into the greater community like a vile destructive virus again. The infection stops here. You are to take this message to mankind. Judgement has been served."

An engulfing light intensified around Toby and he put his hands over his face. He felt a rush of air and glimpsed a view of an expanse his mind could barely contemplate. He became aware of weightlessness and a distant buzzing. He was back on the orbital. A message had been received from Earth.

"Toby, this is Jack Stone. We have sighted more of the alien ships coming into the system. So far we have counted over fifty."

Jack looked up through the window at the alien ship and contemplated his reply.

WE KNEW YOU WERE COMING

Awareness first came in slight, shocking breaths of perception. Without light and without feeling, knowledge of self surfaced from the endless gloom of involuntary sleep to peer outward and test wakefulness. Susan opened her eyes and coughed lightly.

A sickly sweet female voice informed her of her condition. "Waking process complete. Stasis sleep ended. All body systems at optimum."

Lighting in the sleep chamber was still at only ten percent and she strained her eyes to look at her colleagues and judge their waking state. The mirrored stasis fields had deactivated on two of the four other compartments leaving John Harris the ship's communications officer and Tony Parsons the co pilot still locked in their slumber. Susan turned her head and sucked some water from a tube to her left. Her bed lifted from the passive sleep position and folded to hold her in the seated waking posture.

"I hate this part." It was Emily. "It seems like we've been asleep forever."

"Janet how are you?" Susan asked.

"The usual headache."

"You know it's funny but I never seem to have a headache when I wake up from stasis." Emily stated all too happily.

"Thank you Emily." Janet replied as she put her hand to her forehead. "I believe that is the millionth time you have told us that."

Lighting increased another ten percent and Susan lifted her arms to test her balance. Muscles, normally supple and limber moved slowly and with an unaccustomed soreness. But as all was as good as could be expected she tenderly got up from the chair and checked the terminal on John's still activated stasis chamber. An ominous red illuminated the small display. A shocking chill shot through her body. She shouted quickly. "Janet, Emily will you take a look at Tony's status?" She hoped she was reading the information incorrectly and her crewmates would remedy her mistake.

The two girls stepped slowly and carefully out of their seats and moved to examine the stasis display.

"My god, he's dead." Janet said. She gazed at Susan, fearing her response.

"John as well." Susan whispered.

Janet stepped backward and collapsed into her seat, she put her head in her hands and stared at the floor. "John's wife is pregnant, he asked me not to tell you until we returned to Earth but he was going to resign and stay with her." She switched on her intercom. "A.I.?" She waited for an answer and tried again. "A.I. are you there?"

Susan waited a moment and looked at the two girls, it was clear they were all feeling the same shock and sadness. She decided to break the silence and get them moving. It was important to keep busy and dock the ship as soon as possible. "I'm going to register with orbital control. Janet can you check the A.I. core and see why it hasn't responded? Emily will you run a check on John and Tony's stasis chambers and find out what happened?"

The small dome located at the tip of the crew section housed the operations centre for the colossal seventeen mile cargo ship. A continuous control panel circled the room and was divided by six personnel chairs each connected to the floor by a pair of rails. Individual computer sections had automatically activated and awaited their operators.

Susan walked into the room and sat in the pilot seat, she put her coffee in the cup holder and tapped the icon to open the window shields. A dull drone accompanied the slow movement of the heavy protection as it raised into the overhead section. She stopped and stared at the twisting star field. Confused, she hastily brought up the attitude gauge on her main display. The ship was tumbling end over end. She bypassed the failed stabiliser system and manually fired the thrusters, a plume of exhaust gases obscured her view through the window as the rockets ignited and settled the craft onto an even plane.

"Susan?" Janet's voice came through the intercom.

"Yes Janet. How's it look?"

"The A.I. core has corroded down to a solid lump of matter." Janet paused, her quiet thoughtful voice revealed her confusion. "It's so odd, the biojell needs to be replaced every two years but even then it's not because it has started to decay like this. I've never seen anything like it."

"Do we carry spare biojell?"

"Not this stuff. It's way too expensive, the company wouldn't pay for it."

"So is the A.I. totally useless or can we still use it?"

"It will function as a computer and nothing more. Some of the automatic functions we took for granted will now have to be monitored manually."

"Okay well you'd better get up here. The A.I. is not the only problem we have." Susan switched off the intercom and moved to the navigation terminal. She looked at the location display to find out how far it was to the Leba Enomi orbital platform. Instead of a complicated set of coordinates she found just a short set of numbers and letters, M31 AndVI.

As a child Susan had spent hours gazing through her mother's small telescope dreaming of the day she would be old enough to travel the heavens. One night she found a bright fuzzy object she didn't think was a star and needed to ask what it was. Her mother said it was the nearest galaxy to our own, Andromeda, M31, and that one day in the distant future it would collide with our own galaxy. Susan looked up at her, worried and apprehensive, and her mother smiled and told her not to worry as it wouldn't happen for millions of years.

"What is it?" Janet had arrived.

"What do you make of this?" Susan pointed at the digits on the navigation display.

"M31? Andromeda. Why have you put those coordinates on there?"

"I didn't. The software has placed us at this position." Susan typed a query on the set of letters and numbers into the terminal. The reply came quickly and shocked the two of them.

M31 - ANDROMEDA. ANDVI - PEGASUS DWARF.

"But our travel time was six months. There's no way we could have covered that much distance." Janet said. She had a shocking thought. "What's the date?"

"Pardon?" Susan sat dazed and confused by the their situation and had lost focus on the moment.

"Can you look up the date?" Janet insisted.

The navigation page reduced in size as Susan brought up the ship's main information page. She read out the date to Janet.

"January 4th, 2615. That's about two hundred and fifty years from now."

"And what is our velocity?" Janet asked.

"One point three three light years per hour."

"If you multiply the velocity by time lapsed what is the distance?"

Susan typed the equation into the terminal, she gazed at the answer and looked up at Janet. "According to this we have travelled a little over two point nine million light years."

Janet slumped into a chair. Her voice came as a whisper. "That would be enough to place us in Andromeda." She looked around the room. "Where's Emily?"

"I'll call her." Susan switched the intercom to general call. "Emily have you made any progress?"

Emily's voice sounded tearful as she replied. "They are badly decomposed. I've never seen anything like it. I thought I would switch off the stasis field and find them looking like they were asleep." She paused, Susan and Janet heard her weeping away from the microphone.

"Emily?"

She didn't respond. The crying continued in a stuttered rhythm.

Susan tried to get through to her. "Emily come up here to the control room. There's nothing more you can do down there."

The crying petered out and she sniffed and few times. "Alright, I'm coming up." The intercom cut off.

Susan moved to the pilot seat and initiated a full systems check. She watched the results flow down her display as the different parts of the ship reported their status.

Janet stood behind her and examined the information for the engineering results. She listed the parts she was most interested in. "We're out of fuel for the main engine, thrusters are Okay, reactors shut down Okay when the fuel ran out."

Susan stopped the list and pointed at the display. "Here. It looks like the A.I. failed just a few days into the trip. The main starboard data link collapsed. That could explain a stasis breakdown."

Emily entered and joined Susan and Janet at the display. She looked at Janet and they exchanged a smile. "Don't worry, I'll be alright." Emily said.

Susan turned her seat around to face the two girls who sat in their own positions. "We have to decide what we are going to do. Personally I suggest we turn around and go straight back where we came from. The only problem is fuel." She turned to Emily. "Can we make up enough Hydrogen for a return journey from the water we have on board?"

"How far do we have to go?"

Janet exchanged a glance with Susan and told Emily of their condition. "We were in stasis for two hundred and fifty three years and we are currently in the Andromeda galaxy close to the Pegasus Dwarf cluster. Two point nine million light years from home."

Emily looked anxiously between her friends. "What?"

"It's true Emily, we're stranded." Susan said.

"They're all dead." Emily coughed and leaned forward. "I think I'm going to throw up." She said.

Janet rushed to collect a waste bag from the sanitation locker in the passage.

Susan bent down and put a sympathetic hand on her friends shoulder. "Who's all dead?" She asked.

Emily looked at her with anger and fear. "Everyone. My family, my friends." She wretched and coughed again.

Janet arrived just in time to hold the bag under Emily's mouth and collect the stream of vomit.

Susan looked at Janet and realised she too was struggling to hold back tears. Ever since their situation had become apparent Susan had resisted her own sadness. So far she had succeeded in containing all the desperate emotions that fought to take control. She realised she could either allow the tide of despondency to overwhelm her or keep her head above the water and find a way home. It seemed her only way of surviving this nightmare was to become a strong point her two friends could rely on. She collected a glass of water for Emily and sat in the navigation seat.

Emily swallowed the drink in one gulp. "I'm going to clean up, I'll be back in a minute." She walked slowly through the door into the passage.

"What do you think?" Janet asked.

"We need to get busy and work out a way back home. Sitting around thinking about what's happened will not help us at all. Clearly stasis can hold us for long enough, if you can work out how much fuel we need we can start converting the water to hydrogen. Once the fuel tanks have an adequate load we can head for home."

"I can tell you now we don't have enough fuel. If we took all the water we have for crew consumption and converted it to hydrogen we might be able to get home in possibly two thousand years. If however we had full tanks we could get home in one hundred and fifty years. Remember our usual trip is done under the most fuel efficient acceleration to save money. Now we can forget that and go for a full burn." Janet said. "Have you looked for a planet near here that might have water?"

"I'll have a look." Susan opened the navigation software and set the system on a full area sweep. The display quickly filled with various sized icons and points of light indicating stars and planetary systems. She typed in some parameters for a search asking for planets capable of holding water. "We're in luck there are three possible. One of them is only twelve light years. Can we do that?"

"Yes. I'll take Emily down to the engine bay, she can help me. It'll help take her mind off things." Janet left the room.

The hydrogen gas fuelled the antimatter reactor which in turn powered the gravity generator. The ship 'floated' across space on a wave of graviton particles expelled through the engine system's fourteen exhausts. The energised field created a sphere of influence that partially bypassed normal space-time constraints. This allowed interstellar travel without massive relativity problems.

Susan cut the engines and let the enormous craft coast into a distant orbit. "We will be parked in a few minutes. You can start the check for water."

Emily initiated the planetary survey. "You know the software we have is very basic. The company never intended this ship to be examining virgin planets." She sat back and watched the results slowly fill the screen. She commented occasionally on the information. "Lots of gold and nickel. Temperature minus eighteen at the poles, forty four at the equator. The planet is eight tenths land, it doesn't really have an ocean just a series of large lakes. The biggest resources of fresh water are on the northern continent." She turned to look at her crew mates. "I think we should head north and collect the water from the lakes close to the mountain range." A shrill continuous tone interrupted her. She returned to the display. "The software has detected signs of civilisation."

"Are you sure?" Susan and Janet joined Emily.

"Yes, it's picking up a lot of evidence. The planet has cities and towns dotted all over it." Emily brought up some images to fill the whole display. "There's no sign of life, zero electromagnetic emissions and the atmosphere is totally clean. No pollutants whatsoever."

"They must have been dead a long time." Susan commented.

Janet stared at the fuzzy screen. "Can you clean up the images?"

"No, sorry. This is the best this ship can do. We'll have to get closer."

Susan put her hand on Emily's shoulder. "It's time to prepare the cargo shuttle, you two go down to the bay, check it over and set it up for a trip to the planet surface. We'll need to attach a water carrying pod. I'll take us into a closer orbit. We'll depart in one hour."

The shuttle dropped from the launch cradle through the bay doors and into open space. A slight dizziness swept across the three crew as the shuttle's own artificial gravity took over from its mother ship.

"I'm going to take a look at the A.I.'s linking substructure before we head down to the planet. There has to be a reason the starboard data link collapsed." Susan manoeuvred the small craft out from under the main bulk of the cargo ship and brought it over the central crew section. Floodlights lit the ship's hull throwing the chaotic construction into sharp relief. Just behind the large A.I. dome a small depression marked the site of meteorite impact.

"Looks something small hit us, right in the wrong place, talk about bad luck." Janet started the video cameras.

Susan slowed the shuttle to a crawl and circled the hole. "Looks like it hit at quite an acute angle. It must have cut right through the cooling system as well." She lifted the craft away from the wounded vessel and accelerated to the planet.

"Susan, there is a massive city roughly one hundred miles north of the equator." Janet leaned over Susan's shoulder and pointed to the location on her display. "If we can land near there I would like to take a look." She asked.

"No problem. I'll put us down on the outskirts. Emily can you find a water source somewhere close to the city?" Susan asked.

Emily looked up from the indistinct image. "There is a river to the west of the city."

#

Susan struggled with the attitude controls. "Emily can you check the starboard thrusters we are losing stability."

"I've got it." Emily reached up and jabbed a finger at the redundancy icons, the symbols remained dark. She activated her terminal, opened the propulsion systems software and bypassed the safety lockouts. The power increased and settled into a steady flow. "Back up's online."

"Looks like the meteor strike damaged more than we thought." Janet said.

"Landing in ten seconds, hold on this may be a bit bumpy."

Susan reduced the power to the landing thrusters and brought the craft down onto the surface. Dust, blasted up by the engines, obscured the surface from view and painted a dirty yellow light across cockpit interior. The engine noise reduced to a distant whine as the three crew shutdown their respective systems. Susan released her safety harness and lifted herself up to get a better view through the small windows. "Not a big river." She muttered.

Emily peered out across the alien desert. "Where's the city?" She asked.

"It starts about a mile behind the hills." Janet replied.

Susan pulled her environment suit from her locker. "As soon as we are pumping water I want to go over to the city and take some pictures and holographic copies." She said.

"I'll come with you." Janet volunteered. "Emily will you be alright monitoring the flow?"

"Yes, I'm not in the mood to have a look over there anyway." Emily pulled on her suit and connected up a small personnel tank. "Call me if you see any aliens."

Susan smiled, she was glad to see her friend's sense of humour returning. "Everyone ready?"

70

Three large pipes snaked from the shuttle's cargo pod to the river and disappeared under the surface. A small gravity impeller located in the body of the craft pulled the water through the conduits into the large cargo pod. Emily watched the digital dials on the exterior of the shuttle and made fine adjustments to the flow more out of boredom than necessity.

Susan reached the peak of the last hill and stopped to take in the view of the vast alien city. From the tall distant skyscrapers to the nearby dwellings every single building was decayed and disintegrating. She found the whole vision astounding and filled with a peculiar beauty the like of which she had scarcely contemplated. And there was something familiar, a feeling or a sight she had experienced before as if only in a dream that disappeared upon waking.

"That's funny." Janet joined her at the summit.

"What?"

"When I look down there at the city I feel as if it's all a memory of some kind, like something that happened to me when I was a very small child and it's now faded."

Susan picked up her camera and recorded the city in a high definition three dimensional file. "I have the same feeling, even though it's in such a bad state I still find it to be a beautiful sight." She walked over the brow of the hill and started the long journey to the bottom and the familiar city.

The two suited astronauts skirted around the edge of the ancient metropolis to find a wide boulevard they had spotted from the top of the hill. Occasional stops to look into various buildings revealed a conurbation completely wiped clean of any possessions or domestic installations. Each building was an empty shell bereft of personality or any sense of family. After stopping many times and finding the same lack of any presence Susan and Janet gave up on inspecting the individual structures and made greater effort to reach the main thoroughfare.

They rounded a three storey building and found themselves facing an impressive ornate gateway. Above the entrance, carved into the stone, several depictions of humanoid alien beings riding horse equivalent creatures covered all the available surface.

"It looks like something from ancient Rome." Janet moved closer to the structure and touched it with her right hand. "It's very similar to marble but without any colour."

Susan lifted her camera. "Can you turn to face me so I can get some perspective?" She took her time capturing several images of both the entire edifice and each separate carving. "Shall we continue?"

Emily was alarmed by a tremendous flash that lit up the sky in the direction of the city. "Susan? Janet? Did you see that?"

"See what?" Susan asked.

"Some kind of massive burst of light. For a moment I thought it was an explosion but if your saw nothing then I guess it was something else."

"We just passed through an enormous decorated gate into the city."

"Well I hope it wasn't a reaction to our arrival." Emily entered the shuttle and brought the science interface up on her display. "I'm going to connect to the ship and ask for another planetary survey. I'll let you know if anything turns up."

The wide boulevard was punctuated by statues of the humanoid race as far as Susan and Janet could see. The tall effigies intoned valour, poise and dignity and impressed upon the two viewers a sense of pride and wisdom. Every figure was different to the last in detail as well as position and on closer inspection tiny marks in the stone suggested a sculptor at work.

Susan lifted her camera and recorded each figure as they passed. "They look so human. I wonder what happened to them."

Janet crossed to the closest building and looked inside. "This one is as empty as the rest…" She stopped talking as her radio activated. It was Emily.

"There is a massive electromagnetic emission ongoing in the centre of the city, about seven miles from your position."

"How is the water level?" Susan asked.

"It will be full in a few minutes."

"Come over and pick us up when the pumping is complete. We'll continue looking around here." She looked at Janet for conformation as she talked. "Then we can go and investigate."

72

Susan and Janet exited the empty building they were exploring as Emily landed the shuttle in the centre of the boulevard. They waited in the comparative shelter of the doorway while the engines decreased their noisy output and ceased blasting up particles of sand and dirt. The side door opened and the two explorers made their way inside.

Janet sat at her display and accessed the survey data. "Any change in the electromagnetic disturbance?" She asked.

"Not so far." Emily replied.

"Emily, take us closer to the centre. Janet, if the activity changes or flares up or anything unusual happens let us know." Susan released the catches on her helmet. "Ok, take us in."

The shuttle lifted off the boulevard and twisted to face the centre of the city. Three small flaps opened on the top of the personnel section and an array of finely tuned sensors emerged.

"Are you recording this?" Susan asked.

Emily replied over her shoulder. "The shuttle's basic security array has been recording everything but the quality is low and it has to keep downgrading as the small hard disk fills up."

"I've activated the docking antenna. They may be able to add something to the data as we get closer." Janet said. "We have a basic map of the city from the survey, at the centre there is a large open space, it could be a park or some kind of meeting place. It looks like all the energy is centred there."

Susan brought the map up on her display. "Emily can you take us in and we'll have a look."

Emily lifted the shuttle to a greater altitude and increased speed, the deserted city passed beneath them in a dirty grey blur holding little detail or interest for the crew. Each of the three astronauts watched their respective displays with an intense concentration, searching the ever growing number of details for a clue to the purpose of the energy.

Emily braked hard as the craft came upon the target square at the exact centre of the metropolis.

"All electromagnetic activity has ceased." Janet punched several commands into her terminal. "It's just gone. There is no residual energy anywhere to lock onto."

Three tall elegant statues formed a semi circle at the southern edge of the enormous quadrangle. The shuttle approached them from the rear and slowed to circle them and find a suitable landing spot.

Emily gazed through the window and suddenly cried out. The shuttle made an unexpected sideways pitch as she lost control of the vehicle. Her breathing stuttered as she wept. "I don't believe it." She shouted through her irregular gasping.

Susan quickly brought up the pilot software on her display and initiated an automatic emergency landing. The shuttle dumped itself down on the large marble paving stones and disengaged the engines. She moved forward into the small space next to Emily and held her hand. "What is it?" She asked.

Emily pointed out through the windows at the three massive statues facing the shuttle.

Susan and Janet stared, transfixed by the unbelievable sight.

"It can't be." Janet said.

"Let's get Emily back to the couch and sedate her. We can go outside and investigate further when she is ok."

Each girl held one of Emily's arms and with one combined, determined movement lifted her out of the pilot seat and through the cramped space to the rear of the crew section.

Janet retrieved a readymade syringe from the first aid case and injected Emily with a mild sedative solution. "We're going outside. Will you be alright?"

Emily nodded and put her forearm over her eyes.

After Susan and Janet had sealed their helmets back onto their suits they stepped into the small airlock and waited in silence for the system to cycle through.

As the exterior door opened Susan checked her camera to be sure the battery was charged and there was plenty of memory. "Are you ready?" She asked.

"I don't know if I'd ever be ready for something like this." She replied.

The shuttle was dwarfed by the sheer size of the massive central square and made tinier still by the tall sculptures. The three statues stood over the space as a trio of benevolent observers, their expressions portraying solemnity and love.

Susan walked with Janet away from the shuttle and raised her camera to record an image. "How could they have known?" The question was purely rhetorical.

Each statue was a perfect likeness of one of the three stranded astronauts. Dressed in some form of alien clothing and carrying a book in one hand and holding the other forward in a gesture of invitation. They looked down upon the square with a godlike smile. At the foot of each statue, carved into the plinth, the alien inscription was punctuated intermittently by human words. 'Mother', 'Eternity' and 'Destiny'.

Janet broke the silence. "It's no accident."

"What?" Asked Susan.

"Our being here."

Susan walked in the direction of her statue. "The camera range finder estimates they're five hundred feet tall." She had the feeling of a dreamlike reality, as if what she was seeing and experiencing was outside of normality and would soon cease.

Janet parted from Susan and took the direction toward her own image. "It is odd to be so drawn to them."

Her statement made Susan realise she had almost lost influence over her body, she was getting closer to the plinth and could barely feel her legs beneath her. "I'm losing control." The lightness in her mind intensified and her perspective raised to a point where she looked down upon herself. She reached the pedestal and waited in front of it as if this was a pre arranged encounter. The plaque in front of her dropped down out of sight to reveal a robotic arm. It shot forward at immense speed and stabbed her in the stomach with a tiny blade. Her perception slammed back into her physical body. She collapsed onto her backside and hugged her lower abdomen as if trying to shield herself from the already administered assault. Sleep came as a blessed relief.

Susan awoke slowly and with a severe headache, her stomach wound was covered in a small blood stained bandage. Emily had transported them both back to the ship and placed them in the infirmary. She looked at the ceiling for a short while and tried to piece together her last waking thoughts. The statues, the plinth and the lack of control all came back to her in a flood of wretched memory usurping any hope she had at a pleasant recovery. To her left she heard some heavy breathing and she managed to turn her head without too much pain. Janet lay on the bed opposite, her eyes closed and with the same blood stained bandage on her stomach.

Emily entered. "I'm happy to see you're awake, I was worried for a while you would never surface."

"Can I have some pain killers, my head feels like I spent the night drinking neat vodka."

"Sorry but you'll have to await the results of the blood tests. You were both stabbed by an alien machine, I don't know if any dangerous microbes got into the wound before your suit activated the auto derma sealant." She moved to Janet and checked her medical monitor. "It looks like Janet will be awake soon."

Susan lay still and closed her eyes. "How long until you get the blood results?"

"I'll go and see now. I had to run the tests again because the first results must have been tainted." Emily walked into the adjacent room. "Same as last time." She whispered to herself. "OK, I've got them." She returned to the room with a few pages of print out and sat on the edge of Susan's bed. After looking curiously at Susan she read out the findings. "Everything in your system is fine, in fact it is a little too fine. After such a long hyper sleep I would expect that your body would be slightly off in everything it is required to do. But all your systems have aligned themselves perfectly. Now here is the real odd thing." She paused and looked apprehensively at Susan.

"What is it?" Susan asked.

"According to these results you and Janet are both pregnant."

"That can't be." Susan was angry and confused.

"I have run these tests twice it is unlikely they are wrong."

"Well run them again." Susan shouted and regretted it immediately.

"Yes of course."

"What did she say?" It was Janet, she had turned her head and was looking at Susan. A tear had formed in her eye and it dropped to the floor as she blinked.

"Emily says we are pregnant." Susan replied in a quiet monotone.

Emily returned from the computer and announced the results once more. "I've only run the pregnancy test, it's the same result."

"Can you do a DNA test? Find out who the fathers are?" Janet asked.

76

"I wouldn't know how to do it. Like you I have only the basic medical training needed for a ship like this." Emily picked two syringes from a cupboard. "I can give you painkillers now I know they will be safe." She injected each girl and left the room.

The night Susan had spent in the infirmary had been one of lucid dreams and long waking periods. She dreamt of children and great flowing rivers, of nurturing and travel and the passionate love a parent has for their child. Her waking periods were full of worry and fear of being taken away from this planet, this now certain home. A powerful sense of belonging had taken some form of control over her emotional and logical thought processes. The planet below called to her on a level that both frightened her with its intensity and delighted her with its sense of joy. She had travelled the stars for many years with no real family or friends to return to and now so many light years from Earth she had found something wonderful and warming. Leaving was no longer an option for her and she knew that very soon there would be a confrontation with Janet and Emily.

Janet swung her legs out from the medical bed and sat up. "It's time for some food I think." She announced and dropped herself off the edge of the bed onto her bare feet. She pulled a heavy towel robe around her and left the room.

Susan collected her own robe and followed her through to the small canteen. "I have a need to stay. I can't explain why but I feel this is my home now. Are you with me?"

Janet stopped preparing her food and sighed.

Susan could see nothing of Janet's features as her back was to her but noticed a distinct fall in her shoulders. It was obvious her feelings had been torn in two by the same unfathomable subconscious influence the planet had cloaked Susan in.

"My mind is overrun by thoughts, images and impulses. All of which impress upon me a desire to return to the planet below and make a permanent home. I fear we have been infected by more than a medical exam can reveal." Janet turned to Susan. "Yes, I am with you." Her expression hardened to one of a blind determination. "We must not allow Emily to leave, she has to face her own likeness below and realise the potential this world offers."

Susan was surprised by her own lack of disagreement. Janet's assertion would require them to take Emily down to the planet against her will and even though this would be in opposition to

Susan's natural principals she did not oppose it. The thought excited her and she looked forward to the moment of Emily's meeting with her statue. "We should do it now before the water is converted to fuel."

Emily turned as Susan and Janet entered the control room, she looked at the two of them and smiled. "I'm glad to see you're up. The conversion should be finished by tomorrow morning and we can blast out of here."

Susan smiled sat opposite Emily. "Well I'd like to go back to the city and examine the statues. There has to be a reason they're here."

"Well you wouldn't get me close to one of them. I'll stay here if it's alright with you." Emily replied.

Janet sat down putting Emily between herself and Susan, she reached over and took her hand. "You have to come down and see you own statue, the carving is amazing. A group of craftsman worked hard to create something beautiful, something that resembles you perfectly. How can you turn your back on it?"

Susan could see Emily was becoming uneasy and tried to reassure her. "The conversion will get along perfectly well without you. There is nothing to be afraid of down there."

"Nothing to be afraid of? You two have been attacked and impregnated by who knows what. How can you say it is safe?" Emily pulled her hand away from Janet. "I'm going down to get something to eat, I'll see you later." She left the room after pausing at the door to look back at the two girls.

Susan waited until she was sure Emily was out of earshot. "She's not making it easy, I'm worried we might have to use force." She paused and sighed. "You prepare the shuttle, I'll bring her down and one way or another we'll get her on board." After Janet had left for the shuttle bay Susan collected a heavy sedative syringe from the infirmary and made her way to the canteen. Emily had her back to the door and was sitting with a tray of food in front of her. Her shoulders moved slightly in time with her soft weeping. Susan decided to take the initiative and injected Emily in her neck. She slumped backwards, Susan caught her and slowly eased her onto the floor.

Janet looked back over her shoulder as Susan entered the shuttle flight deck with the unconscious Emily on a medical trolley.

After the two girls had lowered Emily onto the small floor she curled into a foetal position and murmured unintelligibly.

"You injected her?" Janet asked.

"It seemed the easiest thing to do."

The shuttle landed softly close to the three statues, the noisy engines slowly wound down to emit nothing but a soft buzz as Janet left the inducers charged on standby. The exterior airlock door opened and Susan stepped out onto the clear marble expanse. Janet passed through the airlock with Emily on an emergency medical hover trolley. At the edge of the square a movement caught Susan's eye, she gazed long and hard at the position and made out some form of colourful image moving slowly in the heat haze.

Janet joined her and studied the same strange shimmering oddity. "They're coming." She said.

"We had better get her in position." Susan activated the medical trolley and pushed it toward the massive sculpture of Emily. The placard on the front of the plinth disappeared from view as if in preparation. She stopped a little distance from the statue and looked around her at the edge of the grand central square. A large number of moving, unidentifiable beings had populated the greater reaches of the enormous plaza and were moving slowly closer as Emily was lowered into position.

The robotic arm moved swiftly and stabbed Emily as cleanly and precisely as Susan and Janet had experienced before. A small amount of blood leaked from the wound before the suits emergency systems sealed the cut.

Susan felt tears in her eyes as an astonishing elation thrilled her body. The desperate alien thirst she had felt ever since her own encounter with a replica in stone had now been quenched. The tide of relief energised the parts of her that had been drained by depression and stress. She turned to find she was surrounded by a multitude of transparent alien humanoids identical to the creatures depicted in the many statues. The smiles and peaceful expressions conveyed their happiness that the three women had found the planet.

A male in extravagant dress stepped forward and talked in an alien language that somehow was understood easily by Susan and Janet.

"We were told of your coming by the great seers. They knew you would come. We built the statues to beckon to you and bring you to the correct place for impregnation. Our civilisation was decaying and our DNA breaking down after a massive gamma ray burst swamped the planet in radiation. Once we knew you would be here sometime in the distant future we decided that it could be only you that would be our chance to restart our race and once again enjoy this beautiful planet. The children you carry will be the first to be born here for countless millennia. We thank you and we apologise for seizing your bodies but we have implanted a love for this planet within you, a love that has produced a bond that will hold you here forever."

WD 4306873

Printed in Great Britain
by Amazon

42218038R00050